TWO-EDGED VENGEANCE

The Major's word was law in Colton. And the call had gone out to get Jet Cosgrave—the man who challenged the Major's power in the tough cowtown. The man who claimed ownership of the Major's Circle C Ranch. The man who had just killed the Major's pet gunman.

Now the town crawled with hardcases—all of them hunting for Cosgrave. Watching them, Jet Cosgrave saw them converge on the hotel—and he read his obituary in their angry, brutal faces...

Todhunter Ballard was born in Cleveland, Ohio. He was graduated with a Bachelor's degree from Wilmington College in Ohio, having majored in mechanical engineering. His early years were spent working as an engineer before he began writing fiction for the magazine market. As W. T. Ballard he was one of the regular contributors to *Black Mask Magazine* along with Dashiell Hammett and Erle Stanley Gardner. Although Ballard published his first Western story in *Cowboy Stories* in 1936, the same year he married Phoebe Dwiggins, it wasn't until *Two-Edged Vengeance* (1951) that he produced his first Western novel. Ballard later claimed that Phoebe, following their marriage, had co-written most of his fiction with him and perhaps this explains, in part, his memorable female characters. Ballard's Golden Age as a Western author came in the 1950s and extended to the early 1970s. *Incident at Sun Mountain* (1952), *West of Quarantine* (1953), and *High Iron* (1953) are among his finest early historical titles, published by Houghton Mifflin. After numerous traditional Westerns for various publishers, Ballard returned to the historical novel in *Gold in California!* (1965) which earned him a Golden Spur Award from the Western Writers of America. It is a story set during the Gold Rush era of the 'Forty-Niners. However, an even more panoramic view of that same era is to be found in Ballard's *magnum opus*, *The Californian* (1971), with its contrasts between the *Californios* and the emigrant gold-seekers, and the building of a freight line to compete with Wells Fargo. It was in his historical fiction that Ballard made full use of his background in engineering combined with exhaustive historical research. However, these novels are also character-driven, gripping a reader from first page to last with their inherent drama and the spirit of adventure so true of those times .

TWO-EDGED
VENGEANCE

Todhunter Ballard

First published by Sampson Low 1952

This hardback edition 2000
by Chivers Press
by arrangement with
Golden West Literary Agency

Copyright © 1951 by Todhunter Ballard
Copyright © 1952 by Todhunter Ballard in the
British Commonwealth
Copyright © renewed 1979 by Todhunter Ballard

ISBN 0 7540 8106 0

British Library Cataloguing in Publication Data available

Printed and bound in Great Britain by
Redwood Books, Trowbridge, Wiltshire

1

Thirty-six hours out of Kansas City, the Western Flyer of the Kansas, Texas, & Southern nosed through the saddleback of Traymore Pass and started downward in the long looping curves which carried it to the floor of the valley of the brawling Beldos. Following the natural contour of the rippled hills, it took the long string of wooden cars the better part of an hour to make the descent, cross the river, and so reach the town.

Inside the glassed parlor car, with its scroll of gold paint, its thick red cushions, and its ornate swinging lamps, the air was hot and stuffy from the all-day run through the desert hills. At the far end the five cattlemen still labored at the card game which had begun in Kansas and had been uninterrupted, except for pauses to eat, for a day and a half.

The fat man was asleep, his plaid drummer's vest held only by the heavy seal watch chain, his bulging stomach forcing the starched striping of his white shirt between the unbuttoned edges of his vest. His mouth was slightly open, and his thick heavy lips fluttered a little with each exhaled breath.

The girl in the gray glove-silk dress sat straight and rigid against the hot plush of her uncomfortable seat, apparently unconscious of the train's lurching sway over the uneven roadbed, of the heat, or the flies which buzzed with undeterred determination around the swinging oil lamps.

Only Jet Cosgrave seemed fully aware of his surroundings. When they had left the city the car had been well filled, but each yellow painted station had taken its toll, until only eight of them remained. Cosgrave now stretched his long legs and shifted in the seat, trying to ease his cramped muscles as the train cut roughly around the twist-

5

ing curves. He turned his attention to the dust-curtained window.

He was a big man but he appeared deceptively slender because of his height. His face was a little too square to be called handsome, with cheekbones that were almost as pronounced as those of an Indian; but his eyes were startlingly blue, and the hair under the edge of the wide-brimmed hat was corn-yellow. Because of his fairness his skin had reddened rather than tanned with the sun, but long weathering had dulled the redness to a deep mahogany. His lips, which were a trifle thin, were saved from coldness by a mobility that betokened easy laughter. He was a man whose feelings were deep but as subject to change, and as violent and unpredictable as a thunderstorm.

For a long mile the rails ran against a sloping hogback. Below, spread out in panoramic candor, lay Colton, as drab and cheerless and uninteresting as a desert town can be. The railroad bisected it into two uneven parts. Southwest of the tracks lay a jumble of unpaved alleys flanked by Mexican shacks, bordered here and there by Indian hovels; while beyond were the neat squares of the shipping pens and loading docks, empty now, but a silent reminder that in this country the cow was king.

Northeast of the tracks stood the yellow station, with its wooden platform, its switch locks and signal tower, looking miniature even in the telescopic clearness of the mountain air. Behind the station ran the wide dust streak that Cosgrave remembered as Railroad Avenue, and fronting this was a straggling row of cheap stores and cheaper saloons, catering for the most part to the Mexicans and the dusty trail hands who, having corralled their charges in the loading pens, crossed the track for their first drink in days. Backing this row of shabby buildings was the business section of the town; and beyond, against the rising ground at the valley's edge, were the even rows of boxlike white houses belonging to the merchants, the townspeople, and the retired ranchers who, seeking to escape the rigors of range existence, had moved in to take up the doubtful pleasure of urban living.

A corner of Cosgrave's mouth lifted. Five years, and the town showed no change. It sat there uncertainly, without belonging to the landscape, a man-made blot upon the beauty that nature had given to the country, as ugly and valueless as the piles of rusting junk which littered the brush beside the Mexican shacks.

The Larkspur hills, rising in the near distance, lifted their timbered slopes out of the desert dryness and the desert heat. Cool and inviting they seemed, a gateway and a promise of beauty and peace, as they merged gradually with the Munyard Mountains, white-capped, vague, and hauntingly mysterious along the far horizon. No Indian would venture into those mountains, and few white men had sought to clamber up their more remote peaks. It was a land of heavy timber, of rushing streams that hurried through deep canyons only to become lost in the greedy desert sinks to the southwest.

Colton, he thought, sat on the dividing line, where the desert came closest to the green-clad hills. It was spawned by the railroad, fed by the cattle and sheep which grazed the hot plain and worked over the rough slopes to the high mesas of the Larkspurs, and swollen by the mines and timber from the higher mountains.

The town drew upon beauty but had none of its own. The men who lived in the white houses and labored in the stores had no sense of belonging to the land. They were a race apart, looking with equal suspicion at the dashing riders, the Mexican herders, and the hard-rock miners who had drifted in from every state of the East and half the countries of Europe.

Colton had become, of necessity, a troubled melting pot where hatred and greed and uncertain suspicion thrived. It had been so five years before, and Cosgrave doubted that it had changed.

The train slowed in the grip of the hand brakes, but it still had sufficient momentum to carry it over the double bridge which crossed the looping river and to slide comfortably up beside the yellow station.

The card players halted their game. Leaving their cards

and chips upon the table, they swung out for a breath of air. When the attendant lifted the girl's bags from the rack, she followed him down the aisle, carrying her wicker lunch basket in one hand and a bird cage with its unhappy canary occupant in the other. As she passed Cosgrave her gray eyes met his steady stare for an instant; a red flood of color came into her cheeks and then she was gone, hurrying along the narrow aisle to the open platform beyond.

"What do you know?" Cosgrave spoke half aloud. "She actually knew I was on this train. From the way she's been staring ahead these thousand miles, I'd never have suspected it."

He grinned then, with the pleasure that any man experiences when he realizes that he's been noticed by a pretty woman, and came to his feet. So tall that he had to duck his head to keep the overhead lamps from knocking off his hat, he started along the aisle, changed his mind, and returned to the side of the sleeping fat man.

He shook the drummer awake, saying, "Colton, Colton," then turned and headed for the end of the car.

"I should have let Fatty sleep," he muttered. "Done him good if they'd carried him through to Ash Fork and he'd had to walk back."

He grinned at the thought, caught up his heavy treed double-cinch saddle in one hand and the blanket roll and saddlebags in the other. The load weighed almost a hundred pounds, but he carried it easily as he stepped onto the open-end platform and dropped down the metal steps, the tiny cinders grating beneath his boot soles.

The train was long. The engine, panting through its bell stack, lay beyond the tower where water already was being flushed downward into the tank. A dozen Mexicans clambered over the tender or passed up wood from the stacked cords beside the track.

The wooden platform was small, and the parlor car, being the last car of the train, missed the platform's edge by a good hundred feet.

Cosgrave dropped his high boot heels into the soft sandy red dirt. Before him stood the girl, her baggage making a small mound at her side where the bearded trainman had dumped it before walking back to set his flag.

The five card players had already reached the platform and had paused to speak to an old loafer seated on a baggage truck. A dozen other loafers sat idly watching the conductor confer with the station man, then turn at his side and walk forward toward the engine.

Behind Cosgrave the drummer came from the car with a puffing rush, his big sample case swinging ponderously against his clumsy legs. He half fell down the steps, almost landing on Cosgrave's back, his momentum carrying him forward so that he would have sprawled headlong had not Cosgrave thrust out the hand which held the saddle to check his progress.

"Thanks, friend." The drummer set his box-toed shoes firmly in the loose dirt, as if to anchor himself, and dropped the heavy case. His face was so deep a red that it was almost purple. "Hell of a country." He pulled a handkerchief from his breast pocket and sponged his neck. "You can have my part of it."

Jet Cosgrave did not bother to answer, and the fat man's attention centered on the girl. Her back was toward them, her eyes on the station. As they watched, she shifted the wicker lunch basket to the hand which already held the bird cage and tried unsuccessfully to pick up the two portmanteaus.

The fat man said, "Here, here." Ever since they had left Kansas City he had been making futile efforts to talk to the girl. She turned now, and her gray eyes weren't quite as remote as they had been on the train. In their depths Cosgrave detected a mirrored anxiety which might have been uncertainty, or fear.

"I . . . please . . ."

The drummer caught up his sample case in his left hand and hefted one of the portmanteaus in the other. Cosgrave noted with secret amusement that the fat man had chosen the smaller of the girl's cases.

"Grab the other one, cowboy," he said, and struck off briskly, his big shoes slipping in the gravelly footing.

Cosgrave and the girl stared at each other for a long moment, then his thin lips quirked and he was relieved to see an answering smile light her eyes. He draped the saddlebags over his shoulder and, with the blanket roll under his armpit, caught up the second bag.

"Welcome to Colton, ma'am," he said and moved forward, holding pace with her shorter stride.

"Thank you," she said. Her dress was long and she was forced to lift it a little to clear the red dust. The canary's cage tilted as she did so, the tiny bird making angry protest.

She spoke to it soothingly, her face turned downward so that Cosgrave had only a side glimpse of her soft rounded cheek.

She was tall for a woman, yet she carried herself with a ready pride that held no hint of arrogance. She seemed oblivious of the afternoon heat and dust as they walked toward the straggling town. At the platform's edge Cosgrave put down the saddle and offered her his hand.

It was a high step but she made it gracefully. The fat man had set down his load and was again mopping at his face. "Hell of a country. Your pardon, ma'am." It was so obvious that he meant no offense that she gave him a smile of reassurance.

"I don't know how to thank you gentlemen. I'd never have managed without you."

"It's still a long way to a hotel," Cosgrave said.

"They're meeting me, thanks."

It was on the tip of his tongue to ask who was meeting her, but he refrained. His eyes ranged along the platform, covering the loafers and several shirt-sleeved townsmen who loitered in the doubtful shade cast by the station building. He saw no one even looking in their direction.

"At least I can put your gear in the station."

He let his own plunder slide to the worn boards and picked up both her cases. Leading the way, he had almost reached the waiting room when a buckboard swirled up the dusty length of Railroad Avenue and pulled to an abrupt stop beside the platform. There were two men on the seat, and they dropped to the ground without giving a second glance at the blowing horses. Both were dusty, and Cosgrave walked on, his look having shown him that they were strangers to him. He had his foot against the station door when the burlier said:

"Miss Austin?"

"Why, yes." The girl stopped, half turned.

"I'm Prince." The man's voice was low, deep in his throat, as if his vocal cords had been rasped with a heavy file. "The Major couldn't make it. He sent us. We'd have been here sooner but we dropped a reach pin."

Cosgrave had a quartered look at the girl and saw her uncertainty. He stood still, his shoulders a little stooped by the weight of the baggage, his eyes on the newcomers.

The man Prince was thick, with blockish shoulders under his grayish shirt. He wore a string necktie instead of a handkerchief, and the tie had slipped around so that the bow was over his left collarbone. Because of the shortness of his nose and upper lip, his mouth at rest missed closing by the barest margin. He could have been thirty or thirty-five; it was hard to tell; but the eyes which met Cosgrave's stare were slate-gray, and there was a hauteur in them as if their owner were not used to interference.

"Who's this?" His deep voice had a demanding quality for all its grittiness.

The girl looked at Cosgrave a little helplessly, realizing that she did not know his name. "A gentleman," she said. "He carried my bags. The car was at the end of the train, and . . ."

"Take them, Bert."

The man with Prince stepped close to Cosgrave. "All right, fellow." He was wiry and black-haired, and his hair had not been cut for months. His face was narrow and his lips loose and mocking. He apeared to be very young, and there was an innate wildness about him which Cosgrave sensed.

Cosgrave dropped the bags. He used one of his freed hands against Bert's narrow chest, pushing the smaller man back.

"Don't crowd me." The tone was mild but the gesture wasn't.

For an instant the black-haired boy was off balance, caught both by the shove and by surprise at opposition. Then his lithe body settled a little into a crouch, and his narrow long-fingered hand fanned clawlike as it hovered above the well worn walnut stock of his single-belted gun.

"Bert." It was Prince, his hoarse tone cutting across the motionless scene with the sharpness of a whetted knife. "Don't forget where you are."

Some of the tenseness went out of the boy. His eyes, black and round and shiny as glass marbles, examined Cosgrave with careful attention.

"No one puts a hand on me." He said this proudly, as if he were delivering a declaration of independence.

"Put the plunder in the buckboard."

For an instant no one in the little group moved, and the only sound was the chirping of the nervous canary. Prince spoke again.

"I said to put the cases in the buckboard, and help Miss Austin."

The dark-haired boy relaxed. The tenseness seemed to flow from his slim body. His loose lips even parted in what could have been mistaken for a grin. He stooped and caught the handles of the heavy suitcases, straightening with surprising ease. He said, "This way, ma'am," to the girl and moved away.

She hesitated, looking from Cosgrave to Prince but getting no help from either of them. She did not quite understand what had happened.

"Thank you," she said, and followed the boy to the buckboard.

Prince had not moved. His gray eyes studied Cosgrave with thoughtful attention. "There was no need pushing the Kid."

"I don't like to be crowded," said the younger man, "and I don't like his manner."

"Few do," said Prince, and seemed to find his own remark amusing. "But few care to push the Kid either, and fewer live long after they have pushed him." He considered Cosgrave again. "That train's pulling out in a minute. You'd be smart to be aboard."

Cosgrave did not answer.

"If you aren't, it's your business." Prince looked at Cosgrave's unbelted waist. "I can keep the Kid busy until the sun goes down, but after dark his time's his own. I'm not offering advice. I never give advice, but if I'd pushed Bert I'd be out of Colton before evening." He turned then, raising a thick arm in a gesture of departure, and walked to the waiting buckboard, his back very straight, his gait the hobbled walk of a man who did most of his traveling on horseback.

The drummer hadn't spoken since the arrival of the buckboard. He stood now, his mouth a little open, his face a deeper purple, his eyes bulging as if his wilted collar fit too tight.

"Friend," he said, the word bursting from him in a whoosh of pent-up breath, "friend, those men are bad. They're real bad, and they mean what they say. I've been in this country before. They kill a man for a joke. They think it's fun. If I were you I'd get on that train."

Jet Cosgrave did not trouble to answer. His eyes were on the girl in the rear seat of the buckboard. She sat very straight and very much alone, and he was filled with wonder that such a woman should be stopping here at Colton. She belonged to the East, to the big cities with their fashionable homes. She had beauty, refinement, poise, and full womanhood. In his lonely camps he had dreamed of meeting such a girl, without quite believing that he ever would. She stirred him; but almost savagely he put the thought away, for as the buckboard pulled around he saw the deep circle burned in the weathered side of the box. Inside the circle was a C, and he stood staring after the departing rig, wondering what this girl had to do with his uncle.

2

Old Jason's station hack car-ried them the length of Fremont and dropped them before the Banner House.

As he found the half-dollar for the old driver, Cosgrave was conscious of Jason's rheumy eyes searching his face. The driver was a dried mummy of a man, shrunken by desert suns and pickled with Pennsylvania whisky, his voice a husky whisper as he peered down from his seat into Jet's upturned face.

"Ain't I seen you before somewheres?"

"Could be, Pop." Jet turned away, dragging his gear from the hack's boot and trailing the fat drummer into the shaded lobby.

The room was long and fairly dark, the wooden awning which sheltered the board sidewalk cutting out most of the afternoon sun. To their right the open stairway led to the second floor. Beside it squatted the desk with its dog-eared ledger and square board key rack. Ahead of them, at the rear of the lobby, was the door leading to the dining room, and on their left the entrance to the saloon. Nothing had changed. Even the broken cane bottoms of the lobby chairs were no more dangerous than Cosgrave remembered them. He dropped the saddle, blanket roll, and bags at the foot of the stairs and hit the hand bell with one swipe of his broad palm.

The saloon door clicked and Jim Banner hurried across the lobby on his short legs. His thin hair was a little grayer and his bald spot had increased in size, but his steel-rimmed spectacles rode high on his wrinkled forehead as they always had and his arms were protected to the elbows by the same sateen wristlets.

14

He rounded the end of the counter, found a broken pen and, reversing the ledger, shoved it under the fat man's nose.

"Afternoon, gentlemen. Come in on the Flyer?"

"We did," said the drummer, "and believe me, friend, she doesn't fly. A good trotter could beat her any day." He mopped his face, accepted the pen, and wrote in a round flourishing hand, *George Pittman, Eagle & Company, fine watches, Kansas City*. He turned then and handed the pen to Cosgrave.

The hotel man glanced at him, squinting a little in the half darkness. Jet took the pen. Below the salesman's sprawling signature he wrote in a script so neat that it looked like copper plate, *J. Cosgrave, The Dalles*.

Banner turned the ledger. He lowered his spectacles by the simple expedient of wrinkling his forehead until they slipped down to the bridge of his nose, then bent his head as if he were trying to peer over them, and read painfully. His stubby crooked forefinger traced out the salesman's name, then started on Cosgrave. He looked up, startled, blinking like a light-disturbed owl. "Jet! You've grown."

"Some," said Cosgrave, and gave him a looping grin.

The hotel man considered him for a moment, as if not entirely certain, then his attention returned to the ledger. "The Dalles. That Texas?"

"Oregon," said Cosgrave.

"Funny name for a town." Banner had not offered to shake hands. "The Major know you're home?"

"I doubt it."

" 'Tain't smart," said Banner, shaking his head. " 'Tain't a bit smart."

"The Cosgraves," Jet told him, "were never noted for their smartness. Folks might also call us bullheaded. Got a room, Banner?"

The hotel man's hesitation was plain. It was obvious that he wanted to refuse, but after a more careful glance at his new guest he turned to the board and lifted a key from its hook.

"Take 14," he said. "End of the hall." He gave Jet another studying look. "The window opens over the kitchen roof. Handy if you don't want to use the stairs."

Cosgrave nodded solemny. "Always liked windows," he said and turned to gather up his things.

In the room he shut the door and stood for an instant looking at the tired sway-backed bed, the single chair, the bureau with its bullet-cracked mirror, and the washstand. The pitcher was a gaudy hand-painted affair, but the matching bowl had evidently been long broken and replaced by a plain white substitute. He crossed to it, pulled off his coat and shirt, and then plunged his face into the tepid water. The sun was well down, casting long rays across the distant mountain peaks and throwing multi-sized shadows from the grubby half-starved trees that moped here and there along Fremont's dusty length.

He straightened, groping for the towel, and moved to the side window. Below him was the corrugated metal roof of Lambert's store, and across it he had a clear view of the two-storied bank building with its false metal columns and arch-topped windows. Andy Delvine stood at the window facing him, his white goatee showing plainly in the last of the red sunlight, his eyes not on Cosgrave but on something in the street before the hotel which Cosgrave could not see. As he watched, the lawyer turned and vanished from sight behind one of his file cases, and Cosgrave shifted to the rear window.

The hotel man had not lied; the shed roof of the kitchen wing slanted below him, and he could hear a faint rattle of pots and pans and the murmur of women's voices. Beyond was the alley, and across it the rear door of Shorham's Livery, with the big pole corral to the right. A half-dozen horses moved restlessly in the dust or mouthed without hope at the few stray strands of hay that still clung to the lower bars of the feed chute.

A boy, red-haired and thin, came out of the barn, his bare feet brown, his overalls held in doubtful security by a single shoulder strap. He looked upward, saw the man staring down at him, and grinned with quick friendliness. Cosgrave raised one hand. He watched the boy climb the corral fence, weave indifferently between the sluggish horses, climb the far fence, and so disappear up Linden.

A noise behind him made Cosgrave spin, then he relaxed as the door swung inward and he saw the fat salesman, minus tie and shirt, his heavy stomach descending in little riples of flesh.

A hint of annoyance touched Cosgrave's voice. "You shouldn't do that. It's always wise to knock."

The fat man sank heavily upon the bed, which groaned under his ponderous weight.

"Friend," he said, "don't scold a man who's trying to do you a favor. I don't know who you are or why you came back, and I don't wish to know. I've traveled this country for three years and I've learned to mind my business and let other men mind theirs."

"A good practice," Cosgrave said, picking up the saddle-bags and beginning to transfer their contents to the bureau drawers.

"But you were kind enough to wake me on the train, and my old grandmother always said one good turn deserves another. I was in the hall a minute ago trying to get a breath of air, and I heard the hotel man talking to someone down below. I heard him say: 'Jet's back. You'd better let the Major know. I wouldn't want the Major to think I was holding out on him.' "

Cosgrave hadn't turned. He went on emptying the saddlebags. "Thanks."

"Friend," said the drummer, "I'm not being curious. I mind my own business. I sell cheap watches and cheaper jewelry. I'm fat and sloppy and I don't know how to fight. Men pick on me because they think a fat man is fair sport, and women take my money and laugh behind my back." He sounded so sad that Jet Cosgrave had the fear he might burst into tears.

"But I like fair play," the drummer went on. "That hotel man pretended to be your friend. He put you in this corner room, so you had the window to retreat through, and then he double-crossed you and sent word to this mysterious

Major. Who is the Major, friend, or is that too much to ask?"

"My uncle," said Cosgrave shortly, as he emptied the last saddlebag and pitched them into the far corner.

"H'm," said the fat man, and studied Cosgrave's reflection in the mirror. "Then I was wrong. You've nothing to fear after all."

"Nothing," said Cosgrave. He undid the blanket roll and from its center produced a belted gun. He strapped the belt about his flat hips, the worn holster hanging low on his left side, the cartridges gleaming a little in the dullness of the room.

He lifted the gun then, springing the cylinder and changing the loads. Finally he turned and grinned at the seated drummer.

"Nothing at all. But I thank you for the warning and I'll give you one in return. Keep away from me. Don't let them think that you're a friend of mine. Stick to your motto, Mr. Pitman; mind your own business and don't worry about what happens to others."

The grin he gave the drummer robbed the words of any sting. Then he turned out of the door and moved down the hall, leaving Pitman alone, unhappy, and unsatisfied with his thoughts.

3

The treads of the wooden
stairway that led upward to the rooms above the bank were
well worn and splintered by many feet in silent proof that
the citizens of Colton had found much need for Andy
Delvine's legal talents.

Jet Cosgrave climbed them slowly, a smile of quiet
pleasure on his face, as if he wanted to prolong in anticipa-
tion a moment that he had dreamed of for many years. He
reached the top and without knocking pushed open the
high five-paneled door.

The rooms beyond were dusty and crowded with the
collection of a lifetime's labors. A gigantic roll-top desk
was so crammed with papers that it would have been physically imposisble to close it. There was a letter press for
making tissued copies, a law library housed in an assort-
ment of packing boxes stacked one upon another to make
a case, a leather chair with the padding showing along the
cracked edge, and a massive brass cuspidor with a battered
yawning mouth that even the most inaccurate chewer
could hit with ease.

The man who occupied this crowded lair looked like a
small blue-coated spider perched in the center of a tangled
web. His face was so thin and his jaw so pronounced that
it resembled the head of a metal nutcracker. A pointed
goatee thrust out from the bottom of his otherwise bare
chin, and his nose was so long and high-bridged that it
seemed to be actually hooked. The shock of hair was dead
white, but the eyes which came around to meet Cosgrave's
over the top of the littered desk were sharp and blue and
penetrating. They swept the big newcomer with a single
glance, taking in the fresh soft shirt, the absence of a neck-

19

erchief, the high crowned hat, and the California pants worn turned up outside the scuffed riding boots.

"Well?" The voice was as high and piping as that of an outraged woman. "What do you want?"

"Is that a greeting to give a wanderer, Uncle Andy?" There was no blood relationship between them, but for as long as he could remember Jet Cosgrave had called the lawyer Uncle. He was not alone in this; half the children of the town so addressed the little man.

Andy Delvine's heavy white brows came down until they almost masked his sharp eyes. "Who are you? No! Take off that hat!"

Silently his visitor raised the big hat.

"Cosgrave hair." Delvine was talking to himself. "I'd know it anywhere. You must be Jetthorn."

"I must be," said Jet. Replacing his hat on the back of his yellow hair, he settled his bulk into the leather chair, found a cigar in his shirt pocket, and thrust it unlighted between his lips.

"Come back to make trouble." Delvine leaned away and surveyed him. "Grown some, too."

"A little," said Cosgrave. "Matter of six or seven inches. As for the trouble, why do you say that?"

"Promised you would," said Delvine. "Stood on the platform and cursed the Major and me. Swore you'd come back and lift our hair." He ran his old fingers through the mop at the top of his small head. "Always worried some."

Cosgrave's grin told nothing. "A seventeen-year-old's liable to say a lot of things, Uncle Andy. Especially when the two men he's been brought up to trust have just finished cutting his throat."

"Wasn't me," said Delvine. "I'm just a lawyer, Jet. A lawyer operates by the letter of the law; he doesn't write it."

"No," said Cosgrave musingly, "but he writes wills."

"Your daddy wrote that will. It was in his own hand. You saw it yourself."

"Uncle Andy," said Jet, "you're only telling half the truth." His face had lost any sign of softness. "I know my father wrote that will, but he never intended the Major to have the Circle C. He willed it to him, yes; but he meant me to have it. There's a part of this I don't know, something that you and the Major held back."

The little lawyer spat, making the old cuspidor ring. "Can you prove it, Jet? All the world knows is what was written in your father's will. The will left the ranch to the Major, and ten thousand in cash to you, naming a St. Louis bank as agent to pay out the money for your education. I did my part; I put you on the train. I also wrote the school, but they wrote back, telling me that you only stayed two weeks."

"It was like a prison," Cosgrave said grimly, and his face tightened further. "They cooped me up in a narrow room, with another boy, and they made us dress up to eat. The master rapped my knuckles with a ruler when I wouldn't. I licked him before I ran away."

"And while you were gone," the lawyer said, "the hill people tried to take the Circle C. The Major whipped them. He killed some and he drove some out, and he scared the rest into leaving the ranch alone."

Cosgrave nodded. "That's what my daddy expected. When he was dying he said, 'Those wolves are just waiting up in the canyons, waiting to hear of my death.' I know that's why he left the ranch to the Major, but I also know that he intended that it be mine in the end. He said so. He said, 'Don't worry, boy; when you're grown, the Circle C will come to you.'"

The lawyer spread his small hands. "I think you're wrong, boy. I think you misunderstood."

Jet smiled thinly. "No, you don't. You know I'm telling the truth, and the Major will know. My father arranged things somehow for the ranch to come to me, only the Major double-crossed him."

"Do you mean you think the Major will hand you the Circle C?" The little lawyer was curious.

Cosgrave shook his head. "I know the Major too well to expect that, but I intend to have the Circle C and I intend to make him sorry that he betrayed my father's trust. Make no mistake about it, Uncle Andy. I want more than the ranch; I want vengeance. I've had five years of riding back trails, of starving and freezing and hating. No man in the world can hate better than a Cosgrave. You should know that."

"I should," said Delvine and he sounded as angry as an irritated bee. "Ever since I've known your family they've caused me trouble. I hate trouble. I want my old age to be quiet and peaceful and undisturbed."

Jet did not smile. "It won't be," he promised. "I've bought the Newmark place. I'm back to stay."

If he had exploded a bomb beneath the little lawyer's nose, Delvine could not have been more excited. "The Newmark place?" Delvine came erect from his desk chair as if it had turned hot. "Are you crazy? There's isn't any Newmark. The Major ran Hal Newmark out of the country four years ago. Newmark made the mistake of siding with the hill people in the fight. When they lost, he ran."

"I know all that." Jet was unaffected. "I met Hal in Oregon last summer. He tried to kill me when I told him who I was. After he calmed down, I bought his ranch."

Delvine settled back slowly into his seat, as if his small legs lacked the strength to support him. He had started to chuckle, and the chuckle grew to a laugh that shook his shoulders as he slapped his scrawny leg with the flat of his veined hand.

"Damn me! Wait until the Major hears this. The Major was always one to see a joke when it's on someone else, and this is on you, son. You go and pay good money for something the Major already has. I suppose you think it will be easier to get the Newmark place away from him than it would be to take back the Circle C."

"I think it will."

Jet was still not excited. He rose, moved over to the window, and peered out at the street below. The sun was well down, and the town was beginning to stir as the coolness of evening drifted in from the hills to quench the heat left over from the afternoon. The lamps in the Palace Saloon across the street were being lit, the Last Chance showed light from the next block, and the hitch rails along the raised sidewalks were filling up with the tired mounts of early arrivals.

He turned back, somber and a little brooding, and then he smiled. It was the same smile which had deceived the Portland gamblers and the hard cases around Laramie, and it might have deceived the small lawyer had it not reminded him of Jet's father.

"You see, Uncle Andy, your law says that I don't own the Circle C, that no matter what my Dad really meant, the ranch belongs to the Major. But the Newmark place is different. I have a bill of sale for the valley, and the taxes have been kept up these last four years."

Andy Delvine blew out his cheeks. Somewhere he had lost his laughter. He said, soberly, "The Newmark ranch-house is now a Circle C line camp."

"That will be changed," Jet assured him. "That will be changed and very soon. In the Newmark, the law—what there is of it—will be on my side. All the Major has is squatter rights."

Looking at him, the little lawyer had his long moment of doubt. The way that Jet carefully uttered each word reminded Delvine more and more of his father, but he laughed.

"Look, boy. I was with your daddy the night you were born. He called me his best friend that night. Maybe you don't think that I've been yours."

"I don't," Jet told him soberly. "I know you connived with the Major to take the ranch away from me. I've spent five years thinking about this, Andy, five years of planning and hate. I'll finish with the Major, and then I'll come against you."

In spite of his control the lawyer's face whitened a little, but he said steadily: "Maybe you don't believe that I've been your friend in the past, but what I'm going to say now is for your own good. The reason the Major drove out Hal Newmark is water. The Little Beldos comes down Newmark Canyon, and flows on to water the Circle C. If you think the Major is going to sit quietly with you astraddle of his water supply, you'd better think again."

"I don't want him to like it," said Jet. "I want him to fight."

"And you'll lose," the lawyer added. "The Major brought in a fighting crew to handle the hill people and he's kept them on, eighteen or twenty riders—which is twice the number your father used. And Cal Prince, the foreman, is as tough as any that you'll find in the Territory."

Jet's eyes lighted with his daredevil smile. "I've met Prince."

The old man looked at him sharply, then went on.

"All you'll get is a fight, and maybe killed. What could you do with the Newmark place, even if you can seize it? You haven't any cows; you don't even own a brand."

"You're wrong," said Jet. "If you care to check at the Territorial capital, you'll find a brand registered in my name: the Circle in a Circle."

He came over to the lawyer's desk, picked up a pen, and drew a circle on a piece of paper; then he drew a C within the circle. He looked around at the lawyer, and his eyes were mocking. He used the pen again, this time connecting the lips of the C so that there were two circles, one within the other. He laid by the pen, stepping back and grinning downward at the small lawyer.

"See?" he said. "You might show my uncle that." He walked to the door, opened it and said, almost as an afterthought: "I don't believe I'll have trouble stocking my range. There must be a lot of Circle C cows already on it. A running iron should do the trick."

He stepped through the door then and moved quietly but quickly down the stairs. Behind him, in the office he had just left, there was utter silence.

4

The office of the Colton
Tribune was a small board building set off by itself a half-block up Linden from Shorham's Livery. Jet Cosgrave used Parker Alley from Fremont, passing two saloons and the garish establishment of Mable Hayes. Two of Mable's girls who sat taking the early evening air on the small porch followed him with their eyes as his boots stirred up little swirls of dust from the alley's rutted surface; but his mind was otherwise bent, and the tinkling strings of the house piano did not penetrate his preoccupation.

Lamps burned in the print shop, and a sandy-haired man with thin cheeks and a straggling mustache bowed above the hand press. He straightened as Cosgrave clicked open the door and looking inquiringly around at his visitor. The red-haired boy who had crossed the corral earlier sat cross-legged at one end of the high counter. His eyes came up and he gave Jet a slow, recognizing grin.

"Hi there."

Jet said, "Hi," and used his boot heel to kick the door shut. "How are you, Allen?"

The printer came forward wiping his ink-stained hands on a greasy rag, balancing himself carefully on his good leg and using the peg as little as necessary.

"Hello." His manner was restrained and careful and withdrawn. Frontier journalism had taught him caution and a clippedness of speech. "Can I help you?"

"Maybe," said Cosgrave. "Your paper still come out on Friday?"

"If the press holds together." There was bitterness and disillusionment in the man's voice. "It doesn't matter

25

much. Few bother to read what I write, and fewer ever pay their bills."

Cosgrave's answering smile held warmth. He could understand the man's misery because he too had known misery and frustration.

"I thought it might be news if you'd print that I've come home. The name is Cosgrave. Probably you don't remember me. I've been away five years."

"Jet! In God's own name what are you doing here?" Allen seized Cosgrave's hand across the counter and squeezed it with both his own. "Man, I'd never known you, never. And yet you look like a Cosgrave; you have the size and the height and the same hair. But I won't publish your news. It would be like issuing your death warrant, believe me."

"It's all over town," Jet told him. "I've talked to Banner and Delvine."

"You always were a fool, even as a kid. Where have you been? Why do you come back?"

Cosgrave started to tell him, as he had told Delvine, but Sam Allen stopped him by turning to the watching boy. "Run on to the house, boy, and get the beans to boiling. Run now, for this is man's talk and not for your big ears."

The boy gave them a disappointed look, but he slid to the floor without protest, his bare feet making no sound as he crossed the worn boards to the door.

When they were alone, Jet asked: "Yours? I didn't know you had married, Sam."

"I haven't," said Allen, and again there was bitterness in his low words. "Who in the devil would marry a man who sports a piece of oak tree in place of a leg?"

"A woman doesn't marry because of a man's legs, Sam."

"And what do you know about women?" The printer sounded savage, then his tone relaxed and his thin face softened. "But the boy is mine, Jet. A trail herd brought him in three years ago and dumped him on the town. He still had an arrow wound in his left shoulder, and the red devils got the rest of his family; but he's too tough for an Indian to kill." The last was said with deep pride. "He's a good lad, Jet; none like him. But you'll see him at supper, for you're to eat with us."

Cosgrave shook his head. "Nothing doing, Sam. It will do no one in Colton any good to seem friendly to me."

"To hell with your uncle." The printer stomped over to put out one of the lights. "The Major may own the Circle C; he may make the other ranchers jump to his whistle and drive the hill people with his gunmen; but he doesn't run this newspaper and he never will."

Jet's lips twisted. "All right," he said, "no need going on the prod."

"I'm not," Sam Allen told him, and grinned sheepishly, "but when I think of the Major and his airs, I get worked up. He's so all-fire high and mighty."

"Like all the Cosgraves."

"Well, yes; at least your daddy was that way. But you never were, Jet."

"You don't know me," Cosgrave told him. "Ask them in Oregon; ask them in the hole-in-the-wall country."

"You've been there?"

"I've been a lot of places, Sam. I was getting ready for something. Ever since I stood on that station platform five years ago, I've been getting ready for something. I'm ready now."

Looking into the sternness of his face, Sam Allen shivered a little. "You'll need help, Jet. I can still shoot, even if this peg keeps me off a horse."

"You can help," said Cosgrave. "You can print the fact of my return. You can put in the paper that I've bought the old Newmark place, that I've registered my own brand."

He talked on, and as he talked Sam Allen's face seemed to grow thinner, tighter.

"You're crazy," he said. "You're forcing the Major to fight. He couldn't avoid fighting you, even if he chose. That double-circle brand is a clear indication that you mean to rustle his steers."

"My steers," Jet Cosgrave said softly.

"Maybe," his friend agreed; "but the law says they belong to the Major. He'll fight, and he has a bunch of hard

cases working for him. They've been getting restless re-
cently—not enough to do. They shot up the Palace two
weeks back, and it cost the Major $1,000 to settle the
damages."

"I've seen hard cases," said Cosgrave, unimpressed.

"You're young," said Allen, "and you're full of hate
and beans, and you didn't lose a leg to a Minié ball at
Gettysburg. See the Major before this gets too far. Don't
soak the Larkspurs in more blood. It might be that you
could make peace."

"The Major wouldn't talk," said Cosgrave.

"He might now," said the printer. "The Major's getting
ready to settle down. He's getting married, some woman
out from Chicago, Illinois."

"So that's it." Cosgrave straightened with sudden interest. "So she's going to marry the Major."

"Who?"

Cosgrave said shortly: "The girl on the train. She came
west with me."

He thought with growing bitterness: That's like the
Major. Every place I turn he has something I want: the
ranch, the girl . . . everything.

Allen did not sense his changing mood. His newspaper
instinct came to the fore. "What's she like, this bride-to-
be?"

Cosgrave thought about her, remembering the long
hours on the train while he had amused himself by watching her.

"She's a lady," he said slowly. "She's used to nice things,
I think, and she has pride. But she can smile and thank a
man with her eyes."

"The Major would want only the best," said Allen.
"Whatever else his faults, he's always taken the best—the
best horses, the best ranch. He'd be the same about
women."

"She's too good for him," said Cosgrave.

Allen looked at him curiously. "You sound interested
yourself."

"Me?" Jet Cosgrave was genuinely surprised, then his

eyes hardened. "You don't understand, do you, Sam? I've never taken time out to look at girls. I have one thing to do, and one thing only: to destroy the Major."

"That," said Allen, "could be a little hard on her, since she's come west to marry him."

"For her own good, she'd better not."

"The wedding is Saturday," said Allen, and limped around the counter. "Consider what you're trying to do, Jet. Vengeance is often a two-edged sword, cutting the user as deep as the victim. Would you like going to the Major's funeral, having to look across his grave at his bride in new-fashioned black?"

"Stop it," said Cosgrave. "You're wasting time. She's a stranger, nothing more; and she has to take her chances at happiness along with the rest of us. She should find out the type of man the Major is before she maries him, and then, knowing what he is, she should be prepared for anything that happens."

"With the Major dead, would you take the ranch from her?"

"It's mine," said Cosgrave stubbornly.

"I'm thinking of you, Jet. Of your future peace of mind."

"Of my conscience is what you mean, Sam. You think I'll never rest easy once I've killed the Major."

"I know it."

Cosgrave shrugged and turned away. "Never mind, Sam. Just print in your paper that I've come home for the Major's wedding. He'll appreciate that. They'll get out the shotguns as a welcome, but the shotguns won't be for the bridegroom."

He left the print shop then and moved carelessly along the darkening street, a big man, yet still boyish in his movements, confident, even a little brazen.

Sam Allen sighed. He limped to the other lamp, blew it out, and stepped from the shop without bothering to lock the door. He stood for a long moment of debate in the shadowed entry, his eyes following Cosgrave as Jet turned into Parker Alley, then regretfully he swung about on the wooden peg and limped the other way, toward his hillside house where the boy was already setting the steaming dish of red beans on the bare top of the deal table.

Jet did not look back as he turned into the alley. When he had traversed it a few minutes before, it had been empty except for the girls on the porch of Mable Hayes's house. Now dust stirred beneath the feet of moving men, men who waited for darkness to make their pilgrimage into this backwash of entertainment which was carefully screened from the politer section of the town.

Cosgrave gave them little attention. In the growing night he classified them only by dress. A few were clerks, laboring all day in the mercantile establishments; but for the most part they were riders or hillmen, with here and there a miner, his clothes still stained with the ore in which he worked. None gave him more than a passing hail, and he came out of the eddy into the full stream of Colton's night life, on Fremont Avenue.

The lights of the saloons burned brightly along its six-block length. The hitching racks had filled up with tired horses while their owners joined the motley crowd surging with early-evening purposefulness along the sidewalks, calling their greetings to chance-met friends or ducking through some swinging door for the first sundown drink. Jet ignored the sidewalk and took the center of the street. Thus avoiding the crowd, he reached the entrance to the Banner House.

Supper was already in progress when he entered the narrow dining room. The big table was filled with steady boarders, but there were seats at the smaller tables against the wall. He saw the fat drummer at one of them but steered away from the man, finding a place close to the kitchen door. He ate silently and without relish, consuming the thin steak and watery potatoes with the dogged intent of a man who knows that he must eat to live but whose mind is wrapped deeply in other things.

He faced the crowded room; and while he knew that several of the diners must have recognized him as he came in, none had stepped forward to offer a welcoming hand. The news of his return would be all over Colton now, but his uncle's long shadow cast its warning shade clear across the town. He did not believe that the Major was here. Certainly if the owner of the Circle C had been within riding distance, he would have come in to meet his bride. The real danger, then, ought not to appear until the Major arrived to direct operations against him, and by that time he hoped to be far from town.

He placed a half-dollar beside his plate, rose, and moved through the kitchen to the alley beyond. The cooks and waitresses stared as he passed, but no one tried to bar his exit. As he stepped into the sheltering darkness of the alley, he paused to fire his cigar and then crossed to the rear door of Shorham's Livery.

The wide passageway of the barn was deserted, lighted by a single lantern that hung from a post peg on the right. He traveled its length and turned into the office, which faced Linden. Here a second lantern's yellow light shone on the broken bits of harness which seemed a part of every stable; it also shown down on the old desk and the old man behind it, leathery and tired and soured by many years of renting to the public. The man hardly glanced up as Jet stepped in. His eyes were intent on the tattered catalogue spread out upon his knees.

"The hostler's sick," he said. "You'll have to stable him yourself."

"Who will?" said Jet, and rested his shoulders against the wall beside the door.

The livery man gave him his full attention.

Jet said, "I want to buy a horse, Pop, a good one." His eyes went around the office and took in the rifle in a saddle scabbard. "I'll take the rifle, too, and some shells."

The livery man laid down his catalogue. "Say, who— you're Jet Cosgrave. I heard you'd come back to town."

Cosgrave said nothing, and the old man got out of his creaking chair. He lifted the lantern from its place and held it forward so that the light fell directly into Cosgrave's face.

"You're Jet, all right, only I never figured you'd get so big. You were a runt when you left here."

Still Cosgrave didn't speak, and the old man considered him.

"I've got a horse for you, only he's not for sale. Your daddy set me up in business a long while back. Did you know that? I don't suppose you did. Need a saddle?"

"I've one at the hotel."

"Bring it over. I'll have the horse ready. And get out of town now. It's filling up. A lot of Circle C boys are in; and believe me, they aren't the crew you used to know. The time to ride out is now, while you still can."

Jet nodded. "I'll be back." He stepped out into the barn alleyway and moved along it to the rear door.

Once outside he crossed toward the hotel kitchen, but midway a voice stopped him. The voice was little more than a whisper, yet it slapped against his eardrums with the force of an unexpected bullet.

"Hold on, Captain," it said. "We'd like a word with you."

Jet stopped, his eyes trying to pierce the gloom of the alley. There was small light. Some seeped from the livery barn he had just left, and he knew that he stood framed in it for them to see. A little glow came from the hotel kitchen across the way, and in the dimness he made out a shadowy figure facing him. Then, as his eyes became more accustomed to the darkness, he made out two other men. They had him boxed on three sides.

"Don't move, Captain."

He identified the drawling amused voice now. It was that of the long-haired kid he had pushed on the station platform, the one Prince had called Bert. An anger such as he had never known came up to fill Cosgrave's chest. He wanted to shout with the pressure of it. It was self-directed anger, rage at his own stupidity. He had been so certain of himself, of all his plans. He had been sure that no attack would be made on him until after the Major had reached town. He knew that this attack had not been ordered by his uncle, that it rose solely from the long-haired boy's injured pride. And now all his planning, his five years of waiting, would come to nothing because he had given way to an impulse that afternoon, because he had pushed the baby-faced killer, because he had been hot and tired and the man's demanding manner had annoyed him.

He fought his anger back. If he had any chance at all, he would need a clear head. He felt no fear. He had long ago accepted the premise that some time he would die; and the thought that death might reach him sooner than he expected brought only anger, the knowledge that he would be cheated of his revenge.

He stood motionless, crowding down his fury; and when it was gone he felt cold and empty and detached. He weighed his chances then and found them hopeless. He did not know whether he could beat the boy Bert or not. He thought that perhaps he could. He had a natural aptitude with guns, and it had been bolstered by much practice. But reason told him that they would down him in the end. No man could hope to face three killers, one on each flank, and live.

His eyes had adjusted themselves now and he saw the three clearly. There was nothing to distinguish them from a hundred others in this wide-spaced land. Their clothes were work-worn and dusty, and their hats threw their faces into dark blurs; but their very tenseness warned him that this was not a game. They stood ready to kill him, waiting only for the long-haired kid, who seemed to be their leader, to have his say.

"Captain," he said, and his voice was low, "you pushed me this afternoon. I don't like men to touch me. It drives me wild."

Cosgrave didn't answer and the Kid went on. "You weren't armed then or I'd have shot you down, Prince or no Prince." He spat into the dirt at his feet, as if to show his contempt for the absent foreman's orders. "But you have a gun now. We watched you leave the dining room and we waited for you. Captain, draw that gun."

Cosgrave's left hand almost moved. If he had to die, he might as well take the Kid with him; but in the fraction of a second which it took to crystallize his thought another voice cut across the darkness.

"No, Kid. Not tonight. Don't move, anyone."

Cosgrave disobeyed. He turned his head toward the poles of the corral fence. Standing beyond them, just tall enough so that the rifle she held rested on one rail, was a girl. He had no way of knowing how long she had been there or even what she looked like. Her slim body was a shadow beyond the fence, but her words were as clear and deadly as the rifle barrel that covered his attackers.

These three shifted uncertainly, the gravel dust crackling under their twisting boots.

"One at a time," she said. "Use your off hands and unbuckle your belts. You first, Kid."

The long-haired boy obeyed, cursing in a low monotone. Cosgrave heard the thud as the belted gun struck the alley earth.

"You next, John."

A second thud was heard.

"All right, Plover."

A third gun dropped, and the girl's voice turned mocking and sarcastic. "Three tinhorn badmen. Tell the Major what happened to your guns. Tell him he'll find them hanging at the fork of the Salt Canyon trail; that is, if he has the nerve to send anyone after them. All right, run."

They didn't run, but they did turn and move quickly along the alley toward where it joined with Parker a good block down. Halfway to the corner the long-haired boy paused.

"You were lucky, Captain. You won't be lucky a second time." Then he was gone.

Cosgrave turned in time to see the girl lightly bend through the fence and come forward. As she crossed the beam of light from the hotel kitchen, he had one good look at her. She was hatless and her hair was loose and red. She wore a shirt and tight-fitting denims like a man, and she carried the rifle as freely and easily as if it had no weight. She stooped without speaking and gathered up the belted guns, looped them over her shoulder.

"Stranger," she said, "the Kid is right and you were lucky. I saw them sneaking down the alley and I thought they were planning to bushwhack my brother, so I eased across the corral; but you should be more careful if Bert Ives is on your trail."

He nodded, more amused than chagrined by her words. "I will in future, miss."

"Do that." She turned by him into the passage of the livery barn, and the lantern made her hair look golden.

"Wait," he said. "I haven't thanked you. I don't even know who you are. I'm Jet Cosgrave. I—"

"Cosgrave" She stopped dead, turning, and he saw that her eyes were almost green. "Cosgrave—and I saved you." For an instant he thought she would drop the belted guns, swing the rifle to her shoulder, and shoot him. Then she caught herself.

"My luck," she said, and her tone was deeply bitter. "The only time in his life the Kid was ready to shoot some-one I approved of killing, and I had to stop him. Go on, Cosgrave, go on; but remember, this is your lucky night. Your doubly lucky night." She swung away and left him staring after her until she disappeared into the livery office, still carrying her captured guns.

5

The waters of the west fork
of the Beldos, commonly called the Little Beldos by the
hill people, fell down through a deep groove cut in the rimrock and violently entered a box canyon a good mile in
width. There, where the river lost some of its rushing fury
and took up a meandering course which crossed and recrossed the valley in a series of widening sweeps, Hal Newmark had homesteaded. That had been in the early days,
shortly after the war, and he forted himself in with a stout
log building and a kind of stockade to stand off Indian
attack.

Twenty years had made some difference in these hills.
The Indians had been rounded up, kept in uneasy custody
on their reservations by an unhappy army, and the hills had
filled to an extent that the early settlers would not have believed possible. The Newmark stockade had all but vanished, its logs carried away for other buildings, or sawed
into lengths to feed the hungry stoves. The barns which Hal
had built were falling down, and only the main log house
remained in any sort of repair, used now for a Circle C line
camp, as it had been during the four years since the Major
had run Newmark out of the country.

As far as the country was concerned, the valley was now
Circle C property. The fact that the Major held it without
legal title was a point that most of the ranchers were willing to overlook.

Tobe Aires had occupied the camp alone that night.
Usually there were three and sometimes four riders there,
especially during the warmer months, when the Major used
the high mesas of the Larkspurs for summer feed. Cattle
were always drifting higher in the mountains, and the line

36

riders were forced to maintain a constant battle with their stubborn charges to keep them out of the brush-filled canyons, or to fight off the depredations of the hill people, who were not averse to eating an occasional piece of Circle C beef. But on this morning Tobe was alone. Most of the outfit had gathered at the home ranch or ridden into Colton to catch a glimpse of the Major's future bride.

Tobe was a spare man of about forty, made lean and toughened by long years in the saddle, a silent man, disliked by most of his fellows and therefore singled out by Prince to hold down the line while the rest of the outfit made their holiday.

He yawned in his bunk, having slept well past the daylight rising hour that was normal to his kind. Only the pangs of his breakfastless stomach kept him from turning in his blankets and going back to sleep. He rose, pulling on his pants over the underclothes in which he'd slept. He kicked his way into his boots, then catching up an empty bucket, stepped out toward the spring at the bottom of the yard. He had covered half the distance and stopped to scratch his stomach when the click of a shod hoof on stone made him swing about.

A line of horsemen a dozen strong was just rounding the shoulder of timbered brush that stuck out from the west valley wall almost to the edge of the stockade.

Tobe's eyes were still heavy with sleep, his slow mind not yet alert. His first thought was that there had been some hitch in the wedding plans and that the whole Circle C was for some unexplained reason heading for the line camp. Then he realized that these men were strangers, and his wonder grew. He knew most of the small ranchers of the hill country by sight. They were a ragtail crowd with poor horses and poorer arms, and they avoided the Circle C and all its holdings as they would avoid a plague. Besides, the approaching riders had pack horses, a number of them, heavily loaded, and they were all armed, the rifles showing in the saddle boots.

A wordless warning beat across his mind, and without realizing what he did he dropped the bucket and sprinted back awkwardly toward the log house. The leading rider swerved his mount, cutting across at an angle to head off the running man. Looking around, Tobe saw the rider jerk his rifle free. Tobe stopped running then. He stood still, panting, in the center of the yard, a bearded man in a dirty undershirt, his tousled head bare to the morning sun, his blue eyes squinting as the newcomers rode up and spread their horses so that he was all but encircled.

"What do you want?" Tobe could think of no reason to be afraid, here in the yard of the Circle C line camp. It had been years since anyone in the country had dared to draw a gun against any of the Major's men. But he was afraid. He found something sinister in the trail-taut faces, in the dusty clothes.

The man who had attempted to run him down pushed his horse close and grinned at Tobe. "Trespassing, huh?"

Tobe stared upward. The man hadn't shaved and his heavy face was coated by a thick stubbly black beard to which the dust clung.

"Trespassing?" Tobe gasped for words, his slow mind unable to comprehend what this stranger was getting at. "Trespassing? You're crazy. This is the Circle C line camp."

The bearded one seemed to take this as a poor joke. "You're wrong, friend. This is the Double Circle ranch. You're trespassing. You have ten minutes to load your gear and get out of here."

Still Tobe's mind refused to function properly. Ten minutes to load his gear? The log house was filled with Circle C property. He started to protest, then sensing that the men were drawing in against him, he turned toward the door. But he had no thought of leaving. It wasn't heroism on his part, or even any personal feeling for the Major. He'd been raised in a simple code. The outfit you rode for could do no wrong. You obeyed orders without question, without too much thought. Besides, he'd been left in charge. He entered the house and made directly for the rifle on the wall pegs above the fireplace. He had it down and was turning, pumping a shell into the gun as he turned, when Rankin shot him twice.

He fell slowly, the rifle slipping from his lifeless fingers. His bulk sprawled and lay quiet, his soiled undershirt begining to stain now from the bullet holes in his chest as the men pressing in behind Rankin stared down silently. Only one protested, a man older than the rest, whom they called Curly because there wasn't a hair on his bald head.

"You shouldn't ought to have shot him, Rankin," he told the leader. "You didn't need to shoot him."

"He was going for the rifle, wasn't he?"

"He was, but you let him go back into the house. A man worth his salt would fight for his own outfit. You knew what he'd do when you let him go in."

Rankin's patience was thin. They'd ridden hard through the mountain trails to reach this spot on the day Jet Cosgrave had set. They were bone-weary and their nerves were taut.

"Look, old man. I told Cosgrave not to bring you. I told him you were too old even to swing a skillet. If you don't like it here, ride on. There'll be more killing before we're through."

Curly muttered and turned away. He was old, his spirit wasn't what it had been, and a man was a fool to court Dude Rankin's displeasure. He started for the door, but Rankin's voice stopped him.

"Are you going or staying?"

He thought of the long hard miles they had just traveled. He thought of the cheerless hideout that he had left. He looked at the stout log walls, at the men watching him, no hint of sympathy on their tired faces, and he made his choice.

"I'm staying."

"All right, rustle up some water; get a fire going. Bob, you and Hank catch up a horse in the corral and load this on. Rope him good and turn the horse loose. He'll head back to his home place. Turn out the rest of the stock. You others clean out this gear. We're moving in and we don't want the place cluttered up."

Tired as they were, they turned to with a will, stripping the blankets from the bunks, replacing them with their own. Tobe was mounted for his last ride, his limp body lashed across the saddle on the frightened horse.

That was the way Jet Cosgrave first saw it. As he turned into the trail which led into Newmark Valley, he heard the pound of hoofs. Pulling aside into the brush, he watched the horse and its grisly passenger dash by him along the path, the brand on its hip plain as it went by. He made no effort at pursuit. He sat there, resting from the strain of his long ride by turning a little in the saddle and watching the terrified horse until it disappeared around the curve of the canyon side. Then thoughtfully he urged his own mount forward.

He needed no one to tell him what had happened at the line camp. The message of the lashed body was plain enough for all to read, but he frowned. His last orders to Rankin before they had separated had been to move in without bloodshed if it were possible. His quarrel was with his uncle, not with some forty-dollar cowboy who might chance to be riding line for the Circle C at that particular time. But he put the thought away from him. He had known before he started that his return would mark the signal for open war. He had had this in mind when he recruited Rankin and his men.

The crew Rankin bossed were hard. They'd have to be to stand against the Major and his lot, and Cosgrave had glossed no words when he sought them out in the wilder country of the Tetons. None but the wildest would have followed him; and most of them came not only because he promised them an equal share in half the beef they stole but largely because he had assured them there would be a fight.

Some men seem born to fight, driven by an inner impulse which makes them strive for ascendancy above their fellows. Jet Cosgrave knew that he was not the thinker Sam Allen was, nor had he the education to marshal his thinking into ordered channels. Thinking made you hesitate. It had seemed so simple and clearcut when he had started on this battle five years ago: the Major had stolen the ranch from him, and he meant to have it back. But there was a streak of caution in him which had warned his young mind that it would not be an easy task. He needed training, money and support.

He had bent his life directly to this end. He had trained himself and cultivated acquaintances among the wilder men he had met, knowing that only from them could he draw the help he would need. The meeting with Newmark had been an accident, but one which fitted neatly into his plans. The bill of sale that Newmark had given him lent a certain air of legality to what he planned to do.

The law had not bothered him too much, for in the northern half of this rough Territory there was little law save that which men made for themselves. The Territorial capital was too far away, and the politicians sent out from Washington had their own concerns without bothering about the conflicts of the native ranchmen.

The army kept aloof, preoccupied with the sporadic outbreaks of the Indians, holding themselves above, and not concerned with, civil law.

Each town had its marshal, and there were county officers operating under the doubtful jurisdiction of the local courts. But a man who was strong enough could seize what he could hold, and the only reprisals would come from personal enemies.

Jet Cosgrave turned his horse back into the trail, frowning as he rode, cursing himself for a weakness that he had not known was in him. The shock of seeing Tobe's limp body lashed to the running horse had not worn off. He knew that he alone was responsible for the man's death. Except for him, Rankin would never have entered this country. Not that the line rider meant anything to him, but it was a foretaste of what was yet to come.

These hills had always known violence. Long before the first white man had poked his way into their green canyons, the Indians had used them as a battleground; and later the small ranchers had warred desperately, fighting off the growing encroachment of the larger herds.

As a boy he could remember his father riding out grim-faced, trailed by grim-faced hands. He remembered the black looks of the hill children when he first entered school. He had been almost alone at school, the only child from the big spreads. All the others were from the hills. Three-cow outfits, his father had called them. He had been licked badly on his first day. The Polsen boys ganged up on him. There were five of them, all bigger than he was, all older. They beat him and then carried him to the watering trough and dumped him in. He might have drowned that morning if it had not been for the girl.

Judy Polsen had red hair, stringy and unkempt, and freckles so large they looked like blotches on her thin, hungry face. But she could fight like a boy, and she had sailed into her brothers with a club, driving them away, before she turned and helped him dripping from the trough.

The first day hadn't ended it. The feud had run on through the years. He had tried at one time or another to lick each of the Polsens and had failed, for although he had grown, they had grown more rapidly. They shot up, lean and lank and dangerous, hanging together and spoiling to fight until their name became a watchword in the Larkspurs, and any depredation by unknown riders was laid directly at their door.

They had a father as lean and sinewy as they were, Hans Polsen, whose mustache bristled redly against his bright tanned skin. He rode always with a rifle across his saddle-bow, never trusting the newer six gun with its revolving cylinder.

They lived in a log house far up the Salt Canyon. They kept a hundred cattle and a collection of horses almost as wild as the men themselves. They hunted and trapped and quarreled with any of their neighbors foolhardy enough to come within their range.

Jet had ridden up the canyon at sixteen. He'd been looking for the youngest Polsen boy, the one called Olf, who was just his age but already stood a good head taller. He hadn't found Olf that day, and he knew now that it was fortunate, for the best he could have expected was another licking.

Instead he had met Judy. She'd been berrying and she carried a tin bucket in one hand, her rifle in the other. She must have been fourteen then, or maybe fifteen—he had never been certain of the Polsen ages. At first she had waved him away with the rifle, but seeing him unarmed she had moved closer, and soon they were talking as any two children might. He remembered the day clearly. He had not spoken to her since, not until last night, when she slipped across the corral and put her rifle on the long-haired Bert.

Jet had gone back into the hotel after that, taking his saddle and blanket roll and easing them out the window onto the slanting roof of the hotel kitchen.

It was not fear which made him choose this manner of retreat, but an unwillingness to bring on the fight until he was ready. He had entered the livery stable half hoping that the girl would still be there, but she was already gone. Shorham was alone in the small office.

He spoke without getting up. "Take the black, in the end stall. He's not much to look at but he'll be running when the other horses quit."

Jet said Thanks. He took the rifle from the wall, and then, still with his back to the livery man, asked about the girl.

"She came in here not ten minutes ago," he said. "She'd just pulled me out of a bad box. A kid named Bert and two of his pals caught me flat-footed in the alley. They had me whipsawed to a fare-you-well, but she left without taking my thanks. As soon as I gave her my name, she high-tailed fast."

"And why shouldn't she?" said Shorham. "That's Judy Polsen. You should remember her."

"I remember," Jet said slowly. "She was in school with me. We never had a disagreement, she and I."

"But the Cosgraves did," Shorham said. "The Major had two of her brothers killed, and he'd hang the other three if he could get at them without losing too many men. The

Polsens are the only hill people who thumbed their noses at the Circle C. They eat the Major's beef, and to make it extra plain they bring in the hides with the brands cut out." He was silent a moment, lost in his own bitter thoughts.

"The world's a funny place, Jet. You'd think there was enough earth for everyone, but ever since time began men have been fighting over the choicer bits. Why don't you take that horse and ride out. You're young. You've got the whole wide space before you. If you take the Circle C, someone else will try and take it from you."

"Maybe," said Jet.

"There's no maybe," said the livery man. "It's a foregone fact."

"A man has to fight for something; he has a right to believe in something."

"Why? Do the birds? They lose one nest and they build another."

"But even they will fight if they're disturbed."

"I guess so." Shorham's eyes went back to the catalogue. "Maybe you're right. For seventy years I've tried to figure things out and failed. I guess it's too much to expect you to understand before you're twenty-five. I only hope you live long enough to know as little about things as I do, but I doubt it. I doubt it very much."

6

The ruin of the Newmark place made Jet rein his horse. He remembered it with most of the stockade standing, the barns and outhouses in good repair. He sat at the lower end of the valley for a long moment, then rode on slowly.

The slap of Curly's ax sent echoes out against the valley sides. One of the men was repairing a weak place in the corral, and two others tried to shore up the barn's sagging roof.

His first dispirited impression gone, Jet heeled the horse forward and came into the yard just as Rankin emerged from the house. Jet stepped down, walked the horse to the corral gate, pulled off his gear, and draped the saddle across the fence. Then he slapped the black's rump and watch it pick its cautious way toward the bunched horses at the far end.

He thought, The black knows he's a stranger, and he's like me, feeling his way. He turned, caught up the blanket roll and rifle, and walked toward the house.

Rankin stood just outside the door, his weathered hatbrim shading his heavy face. He had shaved, and without the black stubble he looked younger; but the vicious lines of ruthlessness were more apparent about the corners of his mouth.

"Hi, boss."

He had called Jet that ever since they had made their deal and there was a hint of raillery in the words, as if Rankin made a little fun of him. There was a good ten years difference in their ages, the riding boss being the older. He had carved a flaming name for himself across the northern frontier, and it was this reputation that had lined up most

45

of the crew. They would not have followed the unknown Cosgrave for a single mile, but they put their doubtful trust in Rankin's known leadership and ability.

Cosgrave contented himself with a nod. He dumped his blanket roll beside the log wall and squatted down to roll a cigarette. Rankin joined him and they smoked in silence for a few moments.

"Any trouble?"

Rankin didn't bother to look at him.

"No trouble," he said. "Only one man here. He tried for a rifle, like a damn fool."

"I saw him," said Cosgrave. "The horse passed me at the mouth of the canyon."

Rankin looked at him then, finding something in the younger man's voice that he did not like. "I said he went for the rifle."

"I heard you," said Cosgrave, and had the quick thought that for the instant he had the riding boss on the defensive. It was a new experience, a chink in Rankin's armor which he had not known of, and he put the knowledge carefully away for future need. Handling these men was like sitting in a high-limit game without knowing quite what cards might fall your way. He remembered half-forgotten words that his father had used: "Never push your luck. Sit back; wait for the cards; but when you have them, don't hesitate; dynamite."

He wondered, squatting there, if he should call Rankin's hand, if he should make an issue of the line rider's death and prove to this hard-case outfit once and for all that he was boss. It was a temptation that was hard to down. He'd watched Rankin with a gun. The man was fast, and deadly as a snake, but Jet felt that he was the faster of the two. It was a feeling only, for there was no way of testing it unless they came to a showdown. But he let the moment pass. He said instead: "Get the crew together. I want to talk to them." Then he rose, carried his blankets into the house, and selected one of the bunks.

When he came out, they were gathered in a little knot before him, not hostile, but certainly not too friendly in their manner. He knew that in their eyes he was untried, and that until he had satisfied them by action that he was fit to lead they would receive his orders with reserve. Studying them, he thought: This is a poor bunch for any man to turn loose upon a land.

There were thieves there, and murderers, and men who simply could not tolerate the binding rules of civilization. There was no common loyalty, nothing to hold them in a cohesive group except their greed for gain, their need for protection, and their trust in Rankin.

He considered his words carefully, trying to speak in a language they would understand.

"You're in a strange country," he told them, "and you'll find that most people's hands will be against us. But remember two things. Don't antagonize the hill people, the small ranchers scattered in the canyons around us. They have no love for Circle C, or for that matter for any of the big plains outfits. We cannot count on their friendship, but we have nothing to gain by arousing their enmity.

"And second, we touch no stock that doesn't wear a Circle C brand. We want to isolate my uncle, to make him stand alone. If we strike at all the big outfits, they'll gang up on us and sweep us out of the country. Is that understood?"

They looked at each other, and then they looked at Rankin. The big riding boss said softly, "You told us all this before we started south."

"I know I did." Jet Cosgrave's tone tightened. "I want it understood. We're all in this together, but we must have rules; and you can hold this in mind: I'll personally hang the first member of this crew that breaks them."

They stirred under the lash of his words. They were all proud, and they resented orders in any form. Rankin chose to say mildly, "That's tall talk, boss."

Jet looked at him. "It's talk I'll back up," he said quietly. "And if you're smart you'll help me. We're sitting on a powder keg. We have a chance to win because the Major has made himself thoroughly hated throughout this whole country. No man outside of his own crew would raise a willing hand to help him. But if we anger the other ranchers, if we give them reason to ride against us, then we fall." He stood for a moment looking at the clustered men.

"My uncle's getting married this coming Saturday. It couldn't have worked out better for our purpose. The Circle C has other things to think of besides riding line. That's why it was a mistake to kill that man this morning, and a worse mistake to send his body home. But the harm's done." He turned to Rankin.

"Get the place organized. You'd better throw a fence across the upper canyon so we can use it for a gathering ground. Don't let any man ride the hills alone, and steer away from strangers unless they force a fight. That's all." He watched them scatter into smaller groups, returning to the tasks from which he had called them.

Rankin hadn't moved. He said quietly: "Your words make sense, boss, but there's one thing you have to learn. This crew doesn't take to orders that are crammed down their throats."

Jet looked at him. "Meaning?"

"It would be better," Rankin said mildly, "if you told me what you wanted done and let me handle the men."

For an instant Cosgrave had the impulse to tell Rankin to keep out of things. He had never liked the man, and his dislike was sharpened and made acute by the morning's killing. But he held his peace. It was no time for a quarrel now, no time to split the ranks. Everything he'd worked for and dreamed of was almost within his grasp.

He managed to say levelly: "You're right. From now on you give the crew their orders. But be governed by what I've said. Our chance of success lies in not angering the hill people; for if we have to retreat we'll be forced to use the pass that you traveled coming in here, and they could easily cut us off if they chose."

"I'm not a fool," said Rankin.

Cosgrave settled to his boot heels. He picked up a stick, smoothed the sandy ground before him, and drew a rough map.

"Here's Colton," he said. "Here's the Circle C home

place." He indicated the other big ranches and pointed out the various hill spreads. "To the north is the Lone Star mine. There's a town here, maybe ten stores. There isn't another store in miles unless you go to Colton, and I prefer to keep out of there for the time being. Tonight Curly and a couple of men can take that old wagon," he indicated it, standing in the yard, "and bring what supplies we need from Lone Star. You came by it on the way through the pass, so he should be able to find it without a guide. Don't push the crew this afternoon; let them have some rest. If you feel like horsing some cattle out of the brush, well and good. Tomorrow we'll build that holding fence." He rose and turned toward the corral.

Rankin watched him, saying in a dissatisfied voice, "Where are you heading?"

Cosgrave spoke without turning. "Over to the Salt. Most of the mountain people don't amount to too much, but the Polsens are different. They're fighters and they're touchy, and they won't like a bunch of strangers riding the brush."

"Leave them out of this," said Rankin.

Cosgrave shook his head. "You couldn't if you wanted to. Within three days they'd know we're here, and they're spooky. I want no trouble with them. I'd rather talk instead. I'd rather let them know that we mean them no harm." He walked away then, without further argument, not looking back until he reached the corral.

Rankin watched him go, the corners of his mouth turning down, then he rose and disappeared into the house.

7

Cosgrave caught up a fresh horse from the *remuda*. After saddling and mounting it, he climbed the hogback that separated Newmark Valley from that of the Salt Fork and dropped down through the trees into the rocky canyon beyond.

He had slept only five hours in the fireless camp he had made outside Colton, and he could have used more rest. But he knew that time was important, that every hour would count in the battle with his uncle. In his plans to take over the Newmark he had forgotten the Polsens, and he might not have recalled them if the redheaded girl hadn't saved him on the preceding night.

As he saw it, both he and her family had suffered at the Major's hands and their common hatred might well make them allies. There was no discounting the fighting ability of the girl's family. With them at his back he would have attacked the Circle C home ranch without hesitation. They were a tough crew, shrewd and dangerous, and always ready for a fight. So were the men that Rankin had brought in, but they were strangers. An overt act on their part could well inflame the whole country against him. It was not that he feared the mountain people, but he wanted no trouble with them to distract his main effort against the Major. The Polsens were not liked; they were not even trusted; but at least they were native to the Larkspurs and as such they had the grudging respect of the other hill people.

He crossed the high plateau between the canyons, seeing here and there a bunch of cattle feeding, fat from the rich summer grass. This was good range for six months of the year, high enough so that the flies were not bothersome.

50

The only trouble lay in the roughness, in the little blind canyons which the cattle used as hiding places. It would take twenty men to comb the brush, and even then they would miss a good share of the stock.

The Polsens and their neighbors were aware of this. They were not above helping the drift of wayward stock, hiding the unbranded calves until the fall roundup had passed.

He smiled, recalling how this practice had infuriated his father. Now that he himself was planning the same thing on a far larger scale, he discovered that he felt a kinship with the hill people which he had never experienced before. It seemed to depend on which side of the fence you happened to be.

The valley of the Salt Fork lacked the green lushness of the Newmark place. Here the stream had cut its way through rimrock, carving a tortured passage between giant boulders two and three times the size of his horse. Little vegetation grew on the barren slopes; and the trail was a twisted snake, footing around boulders or over a shoulder of the canyon wall, rising and falling constantly, but always probing deeper into the hills.

He dropped off the hogback, his horse sliding and slipping in the descent until at last it stood, quivering and sweating on the firmer footing of the floor. He let it blow for a good three minutes before he urged it on, at a walk now, since the going was bad.

Here and there they crossed wet patches where spring water seeped from the rock crevasses to trickle downward toward the rushing river at his left. The bawling stream deafened him, hammering endlessly in the narrow confines of the gorge, churned to whiteness by the rocks over which it ran. The trail climbed steeply for a mile; then the gorge walls shelved off, and he found himself on leveler ground. Here the way branched, the right trace turning across a gravelly ford while the left cut off from the stream into a clump of heavier timber. In the center of the fork stood the snag of an old piñoh, its trunk broken a dozen feet from the ground. From one of the stub branches hung three gun belts, the forty-fives still in their leather holsters.

He stared at the hanging guns, a smile tightening the tiny sun wrinkles at the corners of his eyes. The girl had kept her promise. She'd hung up the Circle C guns at the trail's fork, a dare to the Major and his men to come after them.

He chirped to his horse and swung into the left-hand trail, reaching the timber and plunging into its shadowed depths. He had traveled less than three hundred feet when a voice from his right called to him to halt. He reined in the horse and turned his head, but for the moment he could see no one. Then she rose from a cluster of rocks over which the trees grew thickly, and stepped into sight, her red head bare, her rifle held at ready.

It was Cosgrave's first full look at her, since on the preceding night the lantern light had been flickering and uncertain. Her wild beauty struck him with the impact of a shock.

Enough breeze filtered through the timber to stir her shoulder-length hair, which hung free and unhampered, making her look younger than he knew her to be. Scarcely twenty-five feet separated them, but the freckles which had once so disfigured her were lost in the lustrous tan of her face. She still wore a man's clothes, but her body beneath them was slim and proud, her strong breast unrestricted by the cotton shirt. She stood lightly on one of the rocks, her shoulder against a foot-thick tree that seemed to spring from the rock itself, the rifle held easily, not pointing at him, yet a real and constant threat.

"This is a private trail, Mr. Cosgrave. Have you forgotten where it leads?"

He felt at a disadvantage, sitting on the horse, and swung down, looping his rein across his shoulder but careful not to move his hands in the direction of the belted gun.

"Listen, Judy. You used to call me Jet. You used to be my friend."

Her chin lifted. "That was a long time ago. We were kids. What we did then doesn't matter."

"I think it does," he said. "I'd probably have drowned in that watering trough if you hadn't pulled me out. Certainly your brothers would have killed me."

"I wish they had."

"No you don't," he said. He dropped the rein, letting it trail, and took a slow step toward her. She retreated to a higher rock and the rifle came around menacingly.

"Don't get any closer."

She was as skittish as a wild colt. She might have been a creature of the woods, high-keyed but unafraid, embodying the fierce beauty and freedom of high places.

He took another step, ignoring the rifle centered on his breast. "You saved my life again last night. That makes you own it twice. What kind of person do you think I am that you believe I'd ride this way to hurt you, or anyone who belongs to you?"

"You couldn't." She said this hotly. "You nor any other Cosgrave. The Polsens can take care of themselves."

"I know that." He moved another step and paused to lean against a tree. "I didn't come here to cause trouble, Judy. I came to ask your father for help. He can't hate the Major any worse than I do, and he's suffered no more deeply at the Major's hands."

"My father wouldn't talk to you. Fight your own battles, Jet Cosgrave, and let us fight ours."

"You're like all the rest," he told her. "Seeing you last night, I'd hoped you would be different."

"Why should I want to be different? I'm proud to be a Polsen."

"A grubby hill outfit." He said it casually, yet the words brought angry color into her face. "You're proud, and so are all the other hill people, but think about it for a spell. What have any of you to be so all-fired proud about?"

She started to answer, then checked herself. "Have you had your say?" she asked instead.

"I haven't even started. I'm going to ride on to your place. The only way to stop me is to shoot me out of the saddle. I'm going to have my say for two reasons. First, I've come home and I mean to remain. I bought Hal Newmark's place. I've brought in my own crew and registered my own brand."

She was curious now, and the rifle had dropped a little. "We're neighbors," he said, "and I have no time to carry on petty squabbles with my neighbors for no other reason than that they happen to bear the name Polsen while mine is Cosgrave."

"The Major won't let you stay. The Newmark is his northern line camp."

"It was," Jet told her. "We took it over this morning."

She considered him in silence, trying to judge what it might mean. "And you want our help to hold it?"

"I want nothing." He was growing impatient, a little angry. "Every time I strike the Major, I'm fighting your battle as much as mine. All I ask is that you'll keep off my back, that your brothers will not feud with my men. The hill people have taken a licking twice from the Cosgraves, and both times it was your own fault. You were always so busy squabbling among yourselves that you never presented a united front."

"So you want to beat the Major," she told him. "Well, I don't think it's possible; but if you do, where does that leave us? The Circle C may change heads but it will still be held by a Cosgrave, and we still have the same fight on our hands."

"Not with me," he said. "I won't fight you, Judy. I'd never fight the person who had saved my life twice."

The color came up in her cheeks again, but this time it was not because of anger. Her words, however, remained cool. "I'm sorry, Jet, but we can't trust a Cosgrave. Believe me, it will be better if you get on that horse and ride out of here. If my father found you on this trail, he'd shoot you down."

"Then he'll have to shoot."

Cosgrave's stubbornness was riding him. He swung back to the horse, amused, thinking: She's beautiful, but she's just like all these mountain people, narrow and bigoted. He was still determined to talk to old Hans Polsen. He caught up the rein and was about to step into the saddle when the girl called.

"Wait." She came off the rocks in a little rush, stumbling once in the awkwardness of her high-heeled boots, and was beside him on the trail. "Wait, Jet. Please don't go up there. I don't want you shot, at least not by my family."

He looked down into her eyes, saw her troubled awareness of him, and knew that his own eyes, too, showed quick response. She was young, warm, and very desirable, with her lips a little parted, her eyes shadowed by worry.

His own mouth felt stiff, and he found words difficult. "I'm going to ride in, Judy."

She read his resolve and knew it to be final. "I'll go first then," she said. "My horse is above the bend in the trail. Give me five minutes, then ride up slow. It would be better not to wear the gun."

He shook his head. "It wouldn't work that way, Judy. If I went in with an empty holster, your father would think that I was afraid. I can't have him think I'm afraid or that I'm asking a favor of him, for he wouldn't grant me a favor. The only hope we have is to make him understand that our interests are common, that he has more to gain by listening to me than by shooting me. An unarmed man would never hold his respect."

She considered him thoughtfully. "You always were smart," she said slowly, "and I'm not certain that I like it. Smart men, I've found, are too often dishonest. Still, I said I'd take you in to see Father, and I will." She turned then and walked away from him up the trail.

He watched her carefully until she disappeared from view. Then he mounted and after the promised five minutes again took up the climb.

The way wound for some two miles through thick timber and then came out into a high meadow that was like the Newmark valley in miniature. The creek—for at this height the Salt Fork was little more than a mountain branch —moved slowly between its turf banks, with here and there a deep pool in which he knew trout must lurk. His chief attention, however, was for the small cluster of ranch buildings against the valley's upper rim. The place was typical of most hill outfits. The main buildings were of logs, roofed with homemade shakes because there was not a sawmill closer than Colton. The barn matched the house, and the corral was of peeled poles. Two milk cows, not common to the country, grazed below the house, held from joining the beef animals by long picket ropes. Horses moved in the corral, and somewhere behind the house he heard the rhythmic beat of a hammer against the iron of an anvil.

Here was peace, and he checked his horse to drink in the beauty of the high meadow. He had always loved these glades, even as a boy. Then he had ranged widely, leaving the Circle C with his grub in a blanket roll and camping wherever night would find him. These trips had often lasted for days on end, and his father, who lacked the eye for beauty or the real love his son felt for the hills, had been wont to compare him to an Indian.

Movement before the house caught his eye, and he urged the horse forward, fearing that his momentary halt might be mistaken for hesitation. In the careful game he played, each move and gesture would be studied by the suspicious mountaineers and interpreted from their own viewpoint. He knew them all, narrow and suspicious and reluctant at too much contact with their fellows. They were a close-knit and close-mouthed lot whose lives were little more than eating and sleeping and the animal pleasures which lone men sometimes found in town.

He saw as he approached that the girl stood before the cabin, talking to a figure seated in a split-back chair. He judged that the man was her father, although the distance was still too great to see his face.

He rode on past the grazing milk cows, pulled up beside the corral fence, stepped from the saddle, and tethered his horse. That done, he angled across the yard to where they awaited his approach, scattering a dozen feeding chickens as he advanced.

His guess had been right. Old Hans Polsen sat in his homemade chair looking, with his almost bald head, like a thin-faced eagle. He had aged in the years since Jet had last seen him; but his beaked nose was just as prominent, and under the bushy brows which had once been red but were now a dun-colored white, his eyes were just as sharp and unrelenting.

"We didn't ask you here," he said by way of greeting. The fact that he did not rise, and something in his position, told Jet that the old man could not leave his chair. "You're not wanted here, and if this fool girl hadn't given her word you wouldn't be here. Now speak your piece and get out."

The sound of hammering behind the house had died, and three men now appeared, two from one corner, one from the other. Jet thought: They have me whipsawed, just as the Kid and his friends had me last night.

The girl still held her rifle, carried in the crook of her arm and pressed against her as if she would have been naked without it; but he could expect no help from her here. If anything, she would be on the other side.

He turned first one way and then the other, giving a curt nod to show that he was conscious of their presence, and found that he could not tell them apart. The family resemblance was amazing, as if the three men were triplets instead of brothers a half-dozen years apart in ages. He had never had much liking for any of them and he had none now, but he wondered which of the five brothers were alive and which had gone down before the Circle C attack. None of them said anything. They stood there loosely, yet their very attitude was a hint of violence, waiting for him to speak, ready to listen but giving no help.

He squatted down then, knowing that the action would release the tension. A man who intended to draw a gun would never put himself into so awkward a position. When he spoke, he spoke directly to the seated father, ignoring the watching brothers and the girl as if not conscious of their existence.

"It's this way," he said. "You and I have never been friendly, which is not surprising, and I make no claim that the last five years have changed me in the least; but I do say that our interests have become the same. As long as my uncle holds the Circle C, you live under constant strain, never knowing when he will decide to add Salt Valley to the range he already holds. You're not strong enough to fight him by yourself. If you didn't realize that, you wouldn't sit here when two of your sons have fallen to Circle C guns."

He saw the old man wince at the words, the only sign of feeling he had betrayed. He went on. He told them exactly what he planned. He minced no words. He told them that the crew he had brought in were as tough as any that the Major had employed.

"I'll try to keep them in hand," he said. "I'll order them to stay clear of Salt Valley. But if you should meet any of them in the brush, don't start a war by firing on them, for if you do they'd wipe you out in spite of anything I could do."

"Why should you worry about that?" Old Hans's voice was bitter, festered by old wrongs. "We've never been your friends. I can't imagine a Cosgrave worrying about us."

Why was he worrying about them? It was a question he had been asking himself without finding a proper answer. Maybe it was simply that he did not want to be distracted from his purpose by any secondary wars with the hill people, or maybe it was the girl. Or maybe—here he paused in thought for an instant—maybe he was ashamed at loosing Rankin's horde upon this country. He failed to find his answer, and put the thought aside.

"My motives are of very little importance. I'm only asking that you bear with me until the Major is finished."

"And then?"

He hadn't thought that far ahead, actually. He had been too engrossed with the immediate purpose, with his revenge. He supposed he'd take back the Circle C and run it as his father had. He said so, not knowing what else to say; and the old man laughed, a grating sound, without much mirth.

"And where would we be better off? A Cosgrave would be at the Circle C, and as long as that's true the plains cows will be pushing up onto our grass whenever hot weather kills the low-country feed."

It was the old problem, the problem that had caused the trouble from the first: the rushing streams disappeared into the sandy sinks, and cows could not find enough forage through the summer months unless they were driven into the hills. They were exactly where they were before his coming. He signified this with a shrug, and rose, easing his cramped leg muscles. He could give them his word that once he was in control there would be no more fighting. But who among them would take a Cosgrave's word?

He looked at the old man without reproach and spared a single sweeping glance to include the brothers. "If trouble comes between us," he told them, "it will be none of my making. I've tried to be fair in this. I've laid my cards fully on the table. I can do no more."

He turned then and strode out toward his horse, very conscious of their watching eyes. He wasn't certain that they would let him go, that they would respect the unofficial truce their sister had made. He knew the uncertainty of their tempers and how deeply rooted was their sense of wrong against his family. But he reached the tethered horse without incident, loosened the animal, and swung up before he turned to have his farewell look, raising his hand as he did so in a gesture of salute.

No one of the watching group acknowledged the raised hand. They stood motionless as the rock walls that formed the valley's edge, their eyes upon him, not even speaking among themselves.

He rode out then, experiencing a certain relief when the heavy trees hid him from the ranch buildings. Although he had the impulse, he did not hurry. Instead he held the horse to a steady walk until they had passed through the trees, then he halted, restless and dissatisfied, half mindful to ride back. But he crowded the folly down and dismounted, leading his animal to the right into the sheltering timber, then found himself a seat at the bank of the stream where the water swirled over a two-foot drop into a deep pool.

The grass was a soft spongy cushion over the sharpness of the rocks; and he lay on his back, feeling the tired cramp run out of his muscles, with his eyes on a covey of fleecy clouds which almost imperceptibly sailed across the blueness of the sky.

The chatter and gurgle of the water was as sedative as a lullaby, dulling his consciousness and wiping his mind free of the troubling questions that had assailed it during the last hours. He felt at ease and content, and for the moment washed clean of perplexing doubts. Had he thought, he would have known that this was a dangerous spot, that he was still too close to the Polsen ranch to linger here. But he did linger, almost asleep, with his eyes wide open, until he heard movement and twisted his head.

The girl was above him, looking smaller on the back of her quiet horse. The rifle was unsheathed across the pommel, but it seemed more a natural prop than a threatening weapon. He knew then that he had been waiting for her to come, hoping that she would ride out upon his trail, yet not allowing himself to hope for it consciously.

Her face was set and grave and unsmiling. "For a man who has declared war upon the world, you're wonderfully careless, Mr. Cosgrave."

"Jet," he said. "The name is Jetthorn, as you well know, named for my mother's people who were proud and came from Tennessee."

She ignored the raillery in his voice. "If one of my brothers had come instead of me, you'd be in trouble, Mr. Jetthorn. They were angry at my father for making them hold their hands. They don't like the thought of you in the hills. A line camp at the Newmark place was bad enough, but at least, being a line camp, it marked the northern edge of the Major's operations. But with you making your headquarters there the trouble could be more serious."

He said: "Let's not speak of trouble for the minute. Step down and sit here at my side. There's beauty in these hills which I've never found any place else in the world, and peace and restfulness. When I was younger I used to push into every valley of the Larkspurs. I was an Indian then, slipping through the timber, avoiding men, my own private war party. I've spied on the hill ranchers more than once, without their ever guessing I was around. I've spied on you too, and many times I was tempted to show myself and take you for a recruit."

She was staring down at him, and some of the intense gravity faded from her eyes. "That doesn't sound like you, Jet. You were always so grown-up, so self-contained. Even the day they put you in the horse trough, you didn't cry."

He wiped away her words with an impatient gesture of his hand. "What has that to do with it?"

"That you should have ever played kid games. I don't believe it."

He grinned a little wickedly. "I'll prove it to you, then, I saw you at this very pool one day. You were riding the spotted pony then. You tied him over there where my horse is, and then you stripped and hung your clothes on that stubby branch. I was interested because there were freckles on your back and because you could swim like an otter. I couldn't swim and I was jealous. I think that's the only reason I didn't join you."

He had expected her be angry, but instead she laughed.

"I've still got freckles on my back." She stepped out of the saddle, leaving her horse free to graze across the little grassed patch, its span and reins trailing. She hunkered down like a boy, resting her weight on her boot heels, and catching up a handful of gravel from the stream's edge, let it trickle slowly through her fingers.

"Twice you've surprised me today. First, by riding up this trail and, second, by stopping here. I'm not used to surprises, Jet. I see few people."

Looking at her, he realized how lonely her life must be. Her mother had died when Judy was born, leaving her daughter to grow up in a house ruled by men, without friends or companions of her own sex.

He said in a softer voice: "Why must we be enemies? You must love this country as I do or you wouldn't ride out so much. We stand apart because your name is Polsen while mine is Cosgrave; but besides the names we wear, we're individuals with a right to our own thoughts, our own likes and dislikes."

She puzzled a little, thinking out his words, trying to understand his meaning. "I haven't any friends," she said slowly. "At school I was so much like a boy, playing boys' games, dressing as I do, that the other girls stood apart."

"I'm your friend," Jet told her. "I couldn't be less, since my life belongs to you."

He rose, glanced at the sun, and was surprised to see how low it was. "But I've got to ride. I've got a lot of things to do, things which I can't handle idling beside the Salt Fork."

He offered her his hand and she took it to rise, leaving her rifle lying on the ground. It was the first time she had let go of it in his presence, and he saw in it an omen of the future. Turning, they walked slowly toward his horse.

"Talk to your father," he said. "Make him see that I mean the Polsens no harm."

"Why do you bother?" she asked in real curiosity. "Certainly we have little that you'd want."

When they reached the horse, he unfastened the animal, then turned to look down at her. In that instant their eyes locked.

"Talk to him," he said, not realizing how much his voice had changed. "If nothing else, I'd like to be free to ride up to see you."

Quick alarm jumped into her eyes. "No, Jet, no. If they thought you had any interest in me, they'd hunt you down like a coyote. No, don't go getting any foolish notions into your head."

"They aren't foolish," he told her, catching her shoulders between his big hands. In that moment he knew that he meant everything he said. He bent his head, trying to find her lips, but she struggled away from him, suddenly frightened. He almost lost her, then slipping his big arms about her shoulders, he forced her to him. It was like trying to squeeze a steel spring, for she pressed back from him with all the strength of her arms. But he was too strong. He gradually subdued her resistance until his lips came down against her hot, parted mouth. And then she bit his lip.

In the instant of sharp pain he let her go, tasting the salty blood upon his tongue.

She was away, racing back across the meadow toward the creek. His first impulse was to follow, then he saw that she was headed for the rifle. Swinging up, he spurred his horse around and sent it down the trail at full gallop.

He heard the crack of the rifle behind him even as he felt the tug of the bullet at his hat. He did not slacken but crouched low over the flying horse's neck, trying to look backward under his arm. She stood beside the creek, the rifle still at her shoulder, but even as he looked she lowered the gun.

The little devil, he thought. The deadly little devil. But he did not pull up on the running animal until they passed the fork in the trail and dropped down between the rocky walls of the gulch. Then he slowed and used one hand to lift his hat. The neat bullet hole passed directly through the high crown. Three inches lower and it would have plowed a furrow through his yellow hair.

The little devil, he thought again, staring at the hole with unbelieving eyes. She can handle a rifle; but no one, no matter how good, can place a bullet that accurately when the target is a man on a running horse. She tried to kill me. She most certainly tried to kill me.

He rode on until he reached the point where he had dropped off the hogback into the canyon. The place where he had come down was too steep for ascending, and he was forced to ride a full two miles farther, until he reached a small draw that his horse could climb. Once on the summit of the timbered hill, he broke out into the open for an instant and had a full look at the sun setting far to the west. An involuntary wave of warmth and well-being rose in him. Then, as he turned down into Newmark Valley, his ears were greeted by the rattle of distant gunfire.

For a moment he thought that Judy had gone back after her brothers and that they had come along the ridge by some shortcut known only to themselves. Then he realized that the shots were not from the ridge but from the valley ahead, and that they were increasing in volume. His mouth thinned into a tight line and he spurred his tired horse forward, driving recklessly toward the old ranch buildings.

His crew was attacked, and the attack could certainly not come from any quarter but the Circle C. As he rode he loosened his rifle, wondering if the showdown with his uncle was at hand. The Major was not a man who waited. He might be striking in full force at that minute.

8

The home ranch of the Circle C sat at the mouth of the canyon where the Little Beldos broke out of the hills in its wild scramble to join the larger river.

Here the Cosgraves had settled shortly after the war, driving ahead of them a herd of almost worthless Texas cattle. The cows had multiplied, and the Cosgrave holdings had been enlarged until the brand was seen for miles in every direction from the ranch. Troubled first by Indians and then by the small settlers who crowded into the Larkspurs, they had held their place by sheer force.

Always a fighting outfit, it was now thoroughly feared and hated. The men brought in by the Major to replace his brother's crew were arrogant and reckless and proud. The Major held them with a light rein, asking few questions as long as Circle C was protected from attack. Ruthless himself, he understood ruthlessness in others and turned it to his own advantage. And in Cal Prince he had found the perfect lieutenant. Prince wanted only the power which his position gave, and he was as jealous of Circle C's rights as was the owner.

It was Prince who now came out of the blacksmith's shed and crossed the hard baked yard toward the main house. The Major had ridden in a half hour before, having been absent for two full weeks in the capital, and Prince was coming to make his report. As he stepped into the big house, he had to avoid the Mexican cleaning women who were already converting it from a bachelor's establishment into something more fitting for the Major's future bride, and Prince's mouth turned downward at the corners.

He was a man who had little use for women, having

found most of his pleasures at the gambling tables or across a bar, and the idea that anyone would deliberately harness himself with a wife was beyond his comprehension. With any other man Prince would have voiced his objection, but the Major was the one man he had never talked back to. He tramped along the hall now, turning in at the door of the room which the Major used as an office, and lifted his hat, showing the heavy hair already touched with a spray of gray.

Linton Cosgrave looked up from the big desk. He had the same yellow Cosgrave hair and the same blue eyes that marked all the members of the family. He was also tall; and now that he was in his early forties, he had filled out, putting muscles upon his big bones and making, as the ladies said, a striking figure of a man. Having come directly from the capital, he was still dressed in town-cut clothes, wearing them with as much distinction as he had worn the gray uniform twenty years before. He had a leader's carriage and a leader's demanding ways, and his eyes turned on Prince without warmth.

"Well?"

Prince rolled the wide brim of his hat in his strong hands. "I met her," he said, "and took her to the Colton House. She has the best room, and I told old Appley that you'd skin his hair if he didn't take good care of her."

"Did you explain that the governor had sent for me, that I couldn't get back to meet her?"

"Sure did." Prince nodded to give emphasis to his words. "Told her you'd probably be home today. You don't have to worry about her being lonesome. The town women are flocking around like a bunch of clucking hens. They're all set up about the wedding, making plans and all."

The Major turned back to his desk as if to show that the talk was finished, but Prince said: "There's something else, Major. Your nephew came in on the same train with Miss Austin."

The man at the desk did not move for a full half-minute. His still shoulders under their neat broadcloth looked wide, almost square.

"Jetthorn?"

"Yeah, that's his name I guess. Delvine talked with him. Delvine told me to tell you he was back, but I'd already seen him at the station. He carried Miss Austin's bags from the train."

The Major turned around then, his blue eyes hard and questioning.

"You mean they knew each other?"

"I don't reckon," said Prince. "At least not from what she said. He was just toting the luggage for a pretty woman, like most any gent would do."

Linton Cosgrave wasn't satisfied. "Fool. Why didn't you make sure?"

Prince reddened under the rough edge of the words. No other man had ever talked to him that way and lived; but long ago he had accepted the Major as the boss, and he crowded down his rising resentment.

"I didn't know who he was. I wish I'd known. He had a run-in with Bert on the station platform. The Kid was ready to take a crack at him, but I interfered. I figured you'd want no trouble with Miss Austin there."

"You're damn' right I don't. I want no trouble anyhow. I'll see him. I'll find out what he wants and send him on his way."

"I'm afraid not," said Prince. "I don't know him, since he was gone from here before I came, but judging from his looks he won't be an easy man to push; and Delvine says he came up to the office making threats. He met up with Hal Newmark and bought his place."

The Major was very quiet, but the big fingers of his right hand closed slowly on a paper knife.

"Go on."

"And he's registered a brand, the Circle in a Circle. He drew it out for Delvine and told him to tell you."

"I see."

"He's declaring war," said Prince. "That's what it amounts to. He means to steal us blind. I was thinking of sending some men up to Newmark just in case. We've pulled everyone out of there but Tobe. I've had the boys cleaning up the place and getting ready for the new missus."

"All right, send some of them back; although I don't know what Jet can do alone, and no one in this country will be fool enough to back his play."

"Maybe not," said Prince, "but those hill people are always restless, just waiting for a crack at us. There's one thing more I haven't told you.

"Bert and a couple of the boys boxed this Jet Cosgrave in the alley behind Shorham's Livery. They had him dead to rights, but that redheaded Polsen girl put them under her rifle and took their guns."

"You mean the Polsens are· backing him?"

"Boss," said Prince, "I don't know any more about it than you do. Bert only told me this morning. He didn't know who Jet Cosgrave was and didn't care. Cosgrave pushed him at the station, and you know how Bert is when a man lays a hand on him."

"He's crazy," said the Major. "We ought to get rid of him before we have bad trouble with him. He kills for the fun of it."

"But he's a handy man to have," said Prince, "and we're maybe going to need men like that before we finish with your nephew."

"Let him alone," said the Major. "I'll handle him. He's nothing but a fool kid. He never had too much sense."

"But you aren't going to let him get away with this double-circle business?"

"I'm not going to let him get away with anything. But I don't want trouble in the country right now. My future wife is a city girl. She isn't used to our ways, and I don't want to find myself in the middle of a fight before we've half got to know each other."

Prince's displeasure showed in his eyes. Here was the first sign of weakness he had ever found in the Major, and it was brought on by the woman. He didn't hate her, but he did hate her presence; he felt that after the marriage Circle C would probably never be quite the same.

"About the line camp?" he asked, still dissatisfied.

"Get some men up there, of course, but tell them to

avoid trouble. All I want is for them to hold it until after my wedding. Then I'll handle Jet myself."

Prince knew better than to carry the argument further. He had turned back into the yard and started across it when his quick eyes picked up a rider coming in from the canyon side, a lead horse behind him. A little puzzled, Prince turned, walked toward the corral. That was his first look at Tobe's body, still lashed across the saddle of the horse.

The rider was a small rancher from Bear Creek, and he answered their questions a trifle sullenly, as if he knew that he stood on enemy territory and feared that he might not be believed.

"Saw the horse an hour ago," he said. "Thought the man was sick or something, then got closer and saw what it was."

Prince dismissed him with muttered thanks and sent him to the cookshack. After calling a couple of riders to lift Tobe down, he turned back to the house. The Major was still at his desk, and his tanned face did not alter as he listened to Prince's angry words. It wasn't that Prince had cared for Tobe. In reality he had despised the little man; but Tobe had been riding for the outfit, and it was a direct blow at the Circle C.

"So now we've lost the line camp." Prince paced back and forth. "And it will be all those hill people need to start them rising again."

The Major was unmoved. "That was a silly thing to do, to send Tobe's body in. If he had buried him, or held him prisoner, we might not have known what had happened for a week or two. I never thought Jet had much sense and I guess I was right. Send a couple of men up there to bring him in, or better, go yourself."

"Shall we hang him?"

The Major considered for a moment. "It would be simpler, but maybe we'd better not. Bring him in and we'll turn him over to the marshal for Tobe's murder. You'd better ride."

Cal Prince rode. He needed no urging, and he took five

men with him under the theory that if two men could do the job, five could do it better. They reached the opening of Newmark Valley in the late afternoon and worked their way forward carefully, hoping to take their quarry by surprise.

The first indication they had that the camp was held by more than one man was the number of horses in the corral. Then a rider suddenly dropped out of the brush to the far right, took one look at the group of horsemen, and spurred for the log buildings.

Cal Prince's rifle dropped him three hundred feet short of safety.

Curly had been chopping wood for his cook fire. He dropped his ax and scuttled for cover. Gaining the main house and seizing a rifle, he poked it through one of the windows and fired blindly at the approaching riders.

They fanned out, their bullets hammering against the old logs, searching out the door and smaller windows. Cal Prince rode directly for the corral, his purpose being to release the stock; but even before he reached it he was caught in a murderous cross fire.

Rankin's men had been exploring the valley's edge. Not expecting attack, they had scattered through the timber, combing the little draws for cattle and drifting the growing herd before them toward the house. Their first warning was Prince's shot. They stopped, listening, too widely separated to be sure that the shot had not come from one of their own party. Then Curly's gun took up its hammering, to be answered by the full force of Prince's men.

Rankin was too old a hand to ride blindly into a fight. He pulled his horse around, called to the nearest man, and sent him scurrying along the line. The orders were to drop down off the bench to the timber's edge but not to go charging in until they had some idea of the other force.

Rankin himself rode directly for the house, picking up three of his men along the course. They broke out of the timber in time to see Prince headed for the corral and they laid their shots around him, their angry bullets kicking up little dust puffs about his horse's legs. Prince swung away, not trying to return their fire, and shouted to his riders who were closer to the house. As they turned one went down when Curly shot his horse from under him. He rolled, coming to his feet, and Cal Prince drove toward him, shouting for the man to grab his stirrip.

Rankin had taken in the whole picture at a glance. Made wise in a hundred fights, he knew that the Circle C men must turn back toward the lower end of the valley, and he stood up in his stirrups, motioning to cut them off.

Prince was as conscious of the danger as Rankin was. He swung around, the man on foot running beside him, and angled off across the meadow toward the timber on the other side. Behind him another horse went down, the rider rolling over twice before coming abruptly against a grassy hillock. They reached the stream, only four of them mounted now, and splashed across. As they did so, the man at Prince's side lost his footing and fell heavily into the water. Prince's horse shied away, and the foreman was almost thrown as the frightened animal surged up the slippery bank. A bullet knocked down a man on Prince's right, the riderless horse jumping away as his master fell. At last they reached the line of timber and drove into its screening depths, three men left of the six who had set out. Nor did they check their flight until they had clawed their way up over the rocky ridge and thus come into the canyon of the Main Beldos. By that time all sound of pursuit had dropped away, for, not knowing the country to the east, Rankin had held his men, content to have driven off the attack.

The man who had fallen in the river dragged himself to shore, mud-covered and badly winded. He made no further effort at escape as two of Rankin's riders angled across to cut him off. The other two Circle C riders were dead, and Rankin wasted little time on them.

He sat his horse, looking down on the prisoner, whose wet clothes made him shiver in the evening chill, and threw his questions at the man. There was no need to ask from where the attack had come. The brands on the dead horses were plain to read, but Rankin wanted to know how many had been in the party and what they had hoped to gain.

The prisoner was sullenly scared. A killer himself, he looked for little mercy at these men's hands; also, it was plain from Rankin's face that he would get none. But in that moment, while Rankin had not made up his mind, Jet Cosgrave's horse broke from the timber and he came spurring toward them.

At the sound of his racing horse, the crew swung about, thinking that it might be a fresh attack, and then relaxed as they recognized the rider. Jet's quick glance took in the fallen men, the dead animals, and the sullen prisoner, and he had the full story of the attack.

"How many?" he asked, pulling up beside Rankin.

The trail boss moved his heavy shoulders. "Five or six. They got Jimmy. The damn' fool came out of the trees, where he was safe, and rode for the house. We heard the shot and dropped off the bench. Curly was standing them off." He turned his hard eyes toward the still dripping prisoner. "This one didn't get away."

Cosgrave stared at the Circle C man. "How many were there?"

"Six."

"My uncle along?"

The man lifted his eyes to Cosgrave's face. "If you mean the Major, he wasn't."

"But he sent you?"

The man nodded. "They told us that you'd jumped the line camp and killed Tobe. I got the idea that the Major thought you were alone."

"He doesn't now," said Rankin, and laughed heavily at his own joke. "Get a rope over that tree, Art."

"Wait," said Cosgrave.

Rankin's eyes began to glow dully. "Listen, boss. They shot Jimmy down without a chance. They came here gunning for you."

The prisoner looked at Cosgrave with a gleam of hope. "We weren't to kill you," he said. "We had orders to bring you in and turn you over to the marshal for Tobe's death."

"So you shot the first man you saw," Rankin jeered at him. "Get a rope over that branch, Art."

Cosgrave pulled his horse around so that he stood quartered to the bunched crew. His mouth had settled into a hard line and his eyes were steady, watching them all.

He said calmly: "It's time we had an understanding. I run this show. Any man who breaks orders answers to me."

He saw them stir uneasily beneath the cut of his words and he pressed his advantage. "I brought you here. I planned this for five years, and I won't see it destroyed by a thoughtless act. Killing Tobe was bad enough, but if we hang this man we'll have the whole country on our necks. It's one thing to shoot men down in a fight but quite another to hang a man merely because he's obeying orders." He looked at the prisoner from the corner of his eye, never taking the center of his attention from Rankin and the crew.

Rankin gave no sign that he had heard. He sat so solidly and unmoving in the saddle that he seemed to be a part of the horse. The men behind him watched, ready to take their cue from him. Only Curly, who had walked down from the house, gave the foreman no attention. He still carried the rifle, and his bright cold eyes were on Cosgrave, measuring him as if trying to decide who the winner might be. Cosgrave, his senses alerted by the steady pressure of the waiting men, saw Curly, noted his expession, and judged it correctly.

"Get a horse," he told the cook. "Put this jasper's saddle on it."

"Better not," said Rankin mildly. He looked at Cosgrave. "You have to protect your own crew. You have to back them all the way or they don't have faith in you."

Jet apparently hadn't heard. He said: "If we hang this man, one of you will hang in return; just remember that. We're headed into a fight, and in any fight a lot of people get hurt; but the rules we make at the start will govern this thing. If we hang a Circle C hand, I can promise that the Major will hang a couple of us in return. Do any of you like a rope collar so well that you want to start using one now?"

They stirred again, and Rankins lips turned down. "Hell of a thing, to try and spook your own crew."

"I'm not spooking them," said Cosgrave. "They're big boys now, and none of them are fools. They knew when they rode south that they were riding into war; but there's no need to make it dirtier than we have to by starting a man kicking at the air. Get the horse, Curly."

The cook moved to obey, and Rankin jerked his horse around, as if not willing to remain and see the prisoner ride away.

"Dude!" The word was like the lash of a whip. It halted Rankin and he turned his head.

Cosgrave said coldly: "I'm not used to men riding off when I'm talking to them. Turn your horse back."

For an instant it seemed to the tense crew that Rankin would refuse. He sat blockish and resolute, his back to Cosgrave. Then slowly, as if his unwilling hand moved with no volition from his mind, he sawed on the rein and turned the horse back into its former position.

"You beat a man," he said with deep complaint. "That's no way to belabor your friends, Jet."

"I haven't any friends," said Cosgrave. "There isn't a man here who holds any personal loyalty to me. You all rode south in the hope of profit and for the joy of fighting, and I'll give you both; but the first thing that a man who issues orders has to learn is how to take them. You've never learned that, Dude, but you'll learn if you stay with me. You'll learn or I'll have to kill you."

He was as taut as a drill sergeant. He knew this was the showdown, that he either came out as top dog in this or the whole venture collapsed. He sat stiffly in the saddle, his eyes on Rankin's face, waiting for the trail man to make his decision. If Rankin moved, he would kill him or be killed. If Rankin knuckled under, it would mean that Cosgrave was boss, and that the crew would so accept him.

Rankin weakened. Tough-fibered as the man was, there was a flaw in him that under pressure gave way. He said now, still in his tone of discontent: "Why are we fighting?

What difference does it make if a brush jumper dies, or how he dies?"

Cosgrave said, realizing for the instant that he had forgotten the prisoner entirely: "The difference is that I make the decisions and I expect them to be obeyed. If that's settled . . ."

"It's settled," said Rankin, and pulled his horse around again. This time Cosgrave made no attempt to halt him. He had won. He sensed a certain respect in the watching men that had not been there before.

"Curly," he said, "that horse."

The bald cook walked back to the corral. He roped a horse and saddled it from the fallen animal, then led it back. Cosgrave looked at the prisoner.

The man had straightened now, forgetting his wet clothes in his new hope. He met Cosgrave's look, and there was no meekness in his eyes. He had been saved from death, but he was not one who would offer thanks.

Jet knew his kind and expected none. "What's your name?"

"Sawyer," the man said.

"All right," said Jet. "You can take this message to the Major. I hold this ranch and I expect to hold it. Any Circle C man who comes beyond the canyon's mouth takes his own chances."

"The Major will come," said the man. "He has a lot of cows in these hills, and he needs the summer grass."

"He *had* a lot of cows," Jet told Sawyer, "but from now on the hill grass is closed to him. Ride out before I change my mind."

Sawyer swung up into the saddle. He dared to turn his head and rake the silent riders with his mocking eyes, then he was gone, clattering down the hard-baked trail, his insolence flaunted in the way he rode.

The crew watched him coldly for a long minute, then looked at Cosgrave. He broke the tension by turning to Curly. "It's time to eat. We can't do anything else tonight." He heeled his horse up and about, rode to the corral, and found Rankin against the fence. For a moment they were alone, out of hearing of the others, and Cosgrave used the moment to say: "Any complaints, Dude? If so, now is the time to mention them."

"No complaints," said Rankin. "I've signed on for this and I'll see it through; but after we've finished, then you and I will have a settlement." He turned and walked away. Jet stood looking out over the valley. Sawyer was a dot, moving along the lower trail. He watched idly until the man dropped from sight, then turned toward the house.

Sawyer spurred on across the flatter country toward the Circle C, driving his animal so that he caught the foreman before Cal Prince reached the ranch.

Seeing his dust, they slowed, awaiting his approach, and Prince said sourly, "What kept you?"

Dull anger filled Sawyer, but he held his peace, saying merely: "I guess this is my lucky day. They'd have hung me if young Cosgrave hadn't ridden up in time. He backed Rankin down and—"

"Rankin? Dude Rankin?" Cal Prince had reined his horse.

Sawyer was surprised. "Why, I—"

"Big man, gray in his hair, lined face, little scar under his right eye?"

"That's the man. I saw the scar."

Prince nodded and rode forward in silence. When they reached the yard, he swung down, left his horse, and stalked directly to the Major's office.

"We got licked," he said, as he stepped into the room, his bitterness flooding up in his words. "Your nephew isn't alone. He's got a crew, and Dude Rankin's leading them."

The Major was never one to ask useless questions. He said slowly: "Rankin. I've heard of him."

"And I know him," said Prince. "We came up the trail together to Dodge. He's tough and hard and fast with a gun. It's no wonder we took a licking."

"You're afraid of him?"

Prince said in a low, tight voice: "Some day, Major, you'll go too far. I'm not afraid of any man living, but I like to know my odds when I march into a fight. Dude

Rankin makes them tougher, a lot tougher. It would be cheaper to buy him off."

The Major's eyes narrowed. "Meaning?"

"Meaning that Rankin's gun is always for hire. The only reason he'd buy a piece of this deal is because your nephew must be paying him well. It might be cheaper if we raised the ante."

For a long moment the Major did not answer his foreman. In the ordinary course of events he would have resented the suggestion as a sign of weakness. It was a blow to his pride that any man could be dangerous enough to demand a tribute of any kind form the Circle C, but with his coming marriage he was willing to go to unusual lengths to avoid trouble.

"That's an idea," he said slowly. "But who will get word to him. They'll have a guard out."

"I'll try it," said Prince. "If I can catch their horse guard alone, I'll send him in with word for Rankin. How high can I go?"

The Major drummed thoughtfully on the desk. "As high as you have to. Don't give him the ranch."

"If I know Rankin," said Prince. "He wouldn't want it. That man's fiddle-footed. He likes quick money and long rides." Without further word he left the office, going to the cookshack.

When he had eaten, he caught up a fresh horse and turned back along the river toward the upper valley. Darkness caught him before he reached the lower canyon, but he turned his horse unerringly into the trees, knowing every foot of the rough ground. He circled carefully, certain that no one would detect his approach unless there was a dog, and he had seen none that afternoon. Opposite the ranch buildings he dropped out of the timber and edged forward toward the corral, thankful that the moon had not yet risen.

A flare of light which died almost instantly showed him where the guard was posted beside the fence. He dropped from his horse, trailing the reins, and went forward quietly on foot. His gun was out and pressed against the man's side before the guard had any idea that anyone was near.

The man's sharply drawn breath was the only sound until Prince said quietly: "Take it easy and you won't be hurt. I want to talk to Dude Rankin and I don't want young Cosgrave to know."

The guard didn't answer, and Prince went on: "I'll be at that point of timber behind you. Tell Rankin to come alone. It's dark, but I can tell if there's anyone with him."

"What if he won't come?"

"He'll come. Tell him it's Cal Prince."

The guard rose, and as he did so Prince lifted the man's gun from its holster. "I'll leave this on the fence after you've gone."

Without a word the man turned and moved across the packed ground toward the house. Prince laid the heavy gun on the smooth pole top and faded back to his horse. He had to wait twenty minutes before his sharp eyes picked out the deeper shadow of a man moving across the valley floor, then he hunkered down behind a rock and waited.

When the man was within twenty feet, he called softly, "Sing out, Dude."

Rankin's heavy tones answered. "That you, Cal?" He came on then, his boots scuffing the thin soil. "What's up?"

"Did you get out without young Cosgrave knowing?"

"I did. The whole crew's asleep, all but the guard."

"I'm foreman of the Circle C." Prince had stepped forward. Rankin accepted this in silence. Prince chuckled. "If you'd known I was here, would you have taken this job?"

Rankin's tone was expressionless. "Maybe." He showed no surprise, no curiosity at Prince's visit.

Prince's chuckle deepened. "You always were a cool one. What's young Cosgrave paying you?"

"Half what we steal, to be split with the crew."

"And you figure to get how much?"

Rankin shrugged. "The hills are full of cattle."

Prince knew a sudden blinding rage. This man had at one time been as near a friend as he had had, and here he was coolly planning to steal Circle C beef. Prince's impulse was to pull his gun and shoot Rankin where the man stood, but he knew that the other was watching him equally carefully. He wasn't certain he could beat Rankin, and there was also something else to consider. If Rankin were dead, the crew would take their orders directly from young Cosgrave. With Rankin alive, he might be able to pull them away, providing, of couse, that the prize was worth the doing.

He schooled himself to say: "That's right, the hills are full of beef. What would you think if I told you that the Major would give you some of it?"

Rankin said slowly, "I'd think you crazy."

"I'm not," said Prince. "The Major's getting married to a city girl who doesn't understand fighting. He'd rather pay you off than have a lot of men killed."

"I don't get it."

"Look at it this way," said Prince. "If you stay and help young Cosgrave, we've no choice. We'll have to enlarge the crew and hunt you down. I'm not kidding when I admit it may take days, or even weeks. In the meantime we're barred from our summer range, and the hill people will start stealing on their own hook; but suppose you were to gather a herd, say a thousand or fifteen hundred steers. You can't drive many more over the mountain trail. You'd move out, leaving young Cosgrave alone. You wouldn't have to split your take with him, and what's more I'll promise you a bill of sale for fifteen hundred head."

Rankin said slowly. "I don't believe it. What is it you're hoping for? Let's see the hole card."

"There is none," Prince assured him. "Just pull out the first chance you get. We'll take care of young Cosgrave when you're gone."

The other man was still suspicious, but Prince pulled a piece of paper from his pocket and wrote out the bill of sale. Then he laid it on the rock and without a word turned toward his horse, confident that he had won. Alone, Jet Cosgrave would be an easy target for Circle C guns.

9

As Jet Cosgrave rode away
from her, Judy Polsen raced across the meadow grass like
one possessed, grabbed up her rifle, and hardly realizing
what she did, sent a shot after him. She had no more than
squeezed the trigger when reaction set in and she stood for
one awful moment expecting him to pitch from the saddle. But when he rode on apparently untouched, she
dropped the rifle and buried her face in her hands.

She was a girl not freely given to tears. She had learned
early to withdraw herself, to protect her thoughts in silence.
But she was crying now as she threw herself face down on
the grass. When her sobbing finally ceased, she sat up, feeling suddenly freed from the blinding restraints that had
held her so tightly for so long. She went to the stream and
washed her face, the coldness of the mountain water sting-
ing her hot eyes but also soothing them. Then she looked
at herself, using the Salt Fork as a flexing mirror.

She looked a long time, deciding that her face was too
thin, her tan too deep. Her hair was shoulder-length and
must now be in a wild tangle. She sat back on her boot-
heels, using her fingers as an improvised comb, and murmured aloud: "What can he see in me? What could any
man see in me?" But the memory of his hungry lips against
her mouth was strong. He had kissed her. He had laughed
at first, but afterward the laughter had died from his eyes
to be replaced by something that frightened her.

She was used to men; she had been raised with them,
and her brothers had never been too careful of their talk in
her presence. And on her trips to town she had ridden
across Parker and seen the girls loafing on the veranda of
Mable Hayes's house. But she had thought little of men in

connection with herself. The few stray riders who stopped at the Polsen ranch lacked any attractive features. They were dirty, often hunted men, nervous as mountain cats, very conscious of her brothers and of old Hans seated motionless and forbidding in his homemade chair.

But Cosgrave—Cosgrave was different. Long ago Olf had teased her about him. That was after the horse-trough bath. She could still remember the hated voice and the taunting words: "Judy's got a fella. Judy's got a fella." She had chased him into the woodshed with some well aimed stones, and the memory brought a small smile of pleased remembrance to her face.

Then she rose, picked up the rifle, and strode after her horse. It was a miracle that she had missed. She was as expert as any man with a gun, easily able to knock a chattering squirrel from a tree. Again the feeling of horror seized her. What if she had hit him? What if he'd been hit and was even now lying on the trail? She almost turned her horse downward into the canyon, but a noise behind her stopped her and she spun around in time to see Olf ride out of the timber and cut down toward her.

There was a look on his narrow face that she did not like, and she had the uneasy impression that he might have been behind the tree screen for some time, watching her.

"What are you doing here?"

The feeling between them was a curious one. It was not love. No Polsen seemed to feel any of the softer emotions for other members of his family. It was, rather, a kind of cruel loyalty which bound them together in something that was stronger than love or hate, a tribal feeling carried into these mountains from the barren peaks and high hill country of northern Europe.

"Why shouldn't I be here?"

"The old man wants you." It was a command and he did not amplify it. Swinging his horse, he took the trail upward toward the ranch. They had covered perhaps a third of the distance when faintly, so faintly that it sounded like an echo, rifle shots crackled from somewhere. It was hard to localize the direction. The brush and intervening hogbacks twisted the sound, diffusing it.

Both of them halted and sat very still, then Olf said nastily, "Sounds as if your friend is in trouble."

She flared at him, conscious that her cheeks had reddened and angered because of it, "Watch your tongue."

"You'd better watch your actions," he told her and pushed ahead, pressing his horse into a half-run.

She sat there irresolute, not quite certain what to do. She heard something that might have been more shots, but it was hard to tell above the pounding of her brother's horse upon the trail. Worried, she turned to follow him. But though she spurred, he continued to gain, reaching the yard a good distance ahead of her and dropping from his horse to speak to their father before he took the animal on to the corral. Her other two brothers came out of the cabin, stopping beside her father's chair and waiting as she rode up, their eyes upon her, their faces set in stern and unforgiving lines.

She tried to ignore them, nervous yet unwilling to let them see her nervousness. She rode directly to the corral gate, turned her horse in, dropped the saddle on the top bar with the expertness of long experience, and started for the house, carrying her rifle loosely. She nodded to her father and went to pass his chair, so that she might reach the door, but his hoarse voice stopped her.

"Where have you been?"

It was a question which he never asked. She could not recall that he had ever shown the slightest interest in her movements before.

She came about to face them, conscious that Olf had moved up to join the semicircle.

"Why, down the trail." She tried to sound surprised and yet casual, and as in most such cases she succeeded only in being too casual.

"Alone?"

She knew then that Olf had seen more than she thought, or that his quick eyes had read the signs beside the stream. He was like an Indian, having an almost animal sense of

smell, and she had seen him track a lion for miles across
the rocks. She felt a sudden fear which was entirely foreign
to her.

"I spoke with Jet Cosgrave, if that's what you mean."
Her head was up now, and there was a wild, fearless pride
in her eyes, as if she dared them to question her further;
but it failed to touch the old man in the chair.

"Sven, bring me the whip."

She stared at him, her mouth opening a little. She knew
that this was no idle threat. When she had been younger
she had felt the lash of that whip, as her brothers had felt
it, from time to time. Old Hans had used the lash without
passion, coldly and calculatedly, a chore which had to be
done.

"No," she said. "No."

"Bring me the whip."

She stared at his face, wondering how she had managed
to stay in this friendless house so long, weak with a revul-
sion of feeling for these silent men who were her kin by
blood but who had never given her any sign of being kin
in understanding.

"I've done nothing to deserve being whipped. I talked to
Cosgrave, yes. What is it you're accusing me of doing?"

"Bring me the whip."

Sven laughed, swung into the house, and came out with
the coiled lash in his hand, passing it to the old man.

Hans's sitting position made him awkward, but he drew
back his arm and swirled the whip out, slashing it about the
girl's shoulders, cutting through the thin shirt. She felt
blood start from the burn across her back. She took the
lash a second time and cried out involuntarily, a wordless
protest prompted as much by anger as by hurt. Then she
jumped back, the snaking lash grazing her shoulder. Ignoring the pain, she brought up the gun. "Once more and
I'll shoot you out of that chair." She backed another step
and almost fell, so badly shaken was she with her rage.
"I'm going now. I'm not coming back. Don't try to stop
me."

Her brothers moved as if to cut her off, but the old man

had dropped the whip. He leaned forward, his lips pulled back form his broken teeth, his knuckles showing white as the stubby fingers bit into the arms of the chair. "Let her go. She's no girl of mine. I'll have no wanton in this camp."

She stared at them, at the judgment in their narrow faces, not knowing that she was crying softly, and then she turned and ran to the corral. She would have liked to have taken with her the few trinkets she owned, a brooch which had been her mother's and a heart-shaped locket on a tiny chain, but she dared not enter the earth-floored cabin for fear that they would hold her there.

At the corral she caught up a fresh horse, threw the saddle on its back, and fought the animal as she swung up. No Polsen horse was ever properly broken.

Not one of the men beside the cabin moved. They watched her stonily, convicting her, and she turned away, riding toward the setting sun with the deep knowledge that she would not ride that trail soon again.

She had no clear idea of what she meant to do. Her first impulse was to climb the ridge, to drop downward into the Newmark Valley. She wanted to see Jet Cosgrave at the moment more than she had ever wanted anything in her life, but she put the thought away from her. She did not want to come to him in the whip-torn shirt, with streaks of blood drying on her back.

She rode instead for Colton, driving her horse to a dangerous pace. Usually the hill people detoured the Circle C, but on this night she cut directly across the rolling range, coming within two miles of the big buildings of the home ranch. She met no one, and made the ride faster than she ever had before. At last she pulled her blowing horse into the alley and along it to the livery barn.

10

Sam Allen had worked late
at the print shop, his dead pipe clenched between his teeth.
He was no mechanic, and the workings of the hand press
had always been a baffling puzzle with which he constantly
struggled. Something was always going wrong. No issue of
the paper had ever appeared with smoothness, and he
could never seem to recall from one time to the next how
he had last repaired the press.

He sighed and straightened his tired back as the shop
door opened. He turned and was surprised to see Shorham
coming in with the shuffling gait that always reminded
Allen of a crab. It was such an unheard-of thing for the
old man to leave his quarters at the barn that Allen almost
let his pipe slip from his lips.

"What now?"

Shorham's tone was deeply troubled. "Judy Polsen has
run away from home. The old devil whipped her. He
almost cut the shirt off her."

"So," said Allen and stomped over to the counter.

"She's at the barn," said Shorham. "She came in wanting
to sell her horse."

"And then what does she mean to do?"

"She doesn't know. She talked vaguely of finding work.
She even suggested that I use her as a hostler."

The two men exchanged a long look, then Allen asked,
"What started this?"

Shorham said: "I wormed the story out of her. She
wasn't going to talk but she's some upset, and when I saw
the shape she's in I was ready to ride up the Salt Valley
myself."

"What did happen?"

"Jet Cosgrave." Shorham used the name like an oath. "The young fool rode up there to talk to her family. Coming out, he stopped and she joined him. She told me a lot of silly stuff, about what happened at school long ago, kid stuff. And then he kissed her and she knew the answer to everything. She's in love, Sam. It sounds silly to old fools like you and me, but she's crazy in love. You've got to figure who she is and how she was raised. She's never been to a dance in her life, nor ever been kissed, not even by her pappy, I'd guess. It doesn't occur to her that Jet probably meant nothing except she was a pretty girl and it was a nice fine day."

Allen sucked thoughtfully on his dead pipe.

Shorham gave in to his distress and cursed steadily. "If I had Jet here I'd shoot him dead, so help me."

"Which wouldn't help her," Allen said.

"It wouldn't," Shorham agreed, and his voice gained an embarrassed note. "I was wondering about Nan Ireland. She'd take her in; that is, if you asked her?"

Allen chewed down hard on the pipe stem. "I suppose she would."

"Meaning you won't ask her?"

"I didn't say that." Sam Allen's voice was peevish. "Don't rush a man. Give him some time to think."

"I'll be at the barn," said Shorham. "I don't want to leave her alone too long." He edged out into the dark street, a man so old that his personal cares were of little moment, but not too old to worry about those of others.

In the print shop Allen spread his hands flat against the counter, leaning forward and staring downward without seeing them. He stood there for several minutes, then he turned, blew out the lamps, and limped up Linden in the direction opposite to his own house until he reached a neat picket-bordered yard. He turned in, following the grass-grown flagstoned walk to the three steps, and climbed to the low porch. A neat sign beside the door read *N. Ireland, Dressmaking*. He knocked, heard a woman's steps along the inner hall, and saw the light grow in the window, as she carried a lamp forward toward the door.

"Why, Sam," she said, and pleased surprise lifted her words. She was a small woman, no longer entirely young. Gray shaded the soft amber of her hair, but her eyes were bright and merry. "Come in; you've neglected me too long."

She backed away and he followed her, conscious of the sound of his iron-ringed peg on the floorboards. She shut the door and lighted them along the hall to the rear room, which was both a sitting place and a workshop. A dress frame supported a half-made garment, and the cutting table was covered with bright silk.

"You must be busy," was his comment as he looked at her carefully.

She colored a little under the gaze. "It's the Major's wedding. Everyone in town wants a new dress and no two can be alike. Women are a lot of trouble, Sam."

He remained standing, looking down at her, noting the tiredness in her face. This was a hell of a place for a respectable woman without a husband, he thought. Nothing but work, with no entertainment, little companionship. He knew that it would be the same in any small town, and he wondered why she stayed. With her ability, with her real knowledge of design, she might have done well in the East; she might, perhaps, have become famous and taken a French name. Instead she fashioned dresses for ranchers' wives and the fat hens who had married storekeepers and spent their waking hours clucking their gossip across the back fences of the town.

Some of his impatience broke into words. "Why do you stay in this town, Nan?"

She fitted a thimble, picked up a piece of material, and began her careful stitching, bending a slow smile upon her work. "Why do *you* stay? Your words apply to your case more than mine. You have ability. You might have been a great man."

"With this leg?"

"Sam," she told him quietly, "you're much too sensitive."

"I'm not sensitive." His tone went up a little. "I want

nothing but the best, and a man with a single leg hasn't the best of it."

"You're a fraud. You think you're a philosopher, but your philosophy breaks down when applied to your own cause."

"You've got a sharp tongue," he complained, "and a sharper mind. You skin a man and pick his brains."

"Is that why you avoid me?"

As always he was tempted to tell her why he stayed away, that it was hard to trust himself in her presence; but again he let the moment pass and said instead: "I've come to ask another favor. It seems I always come here asking favors."

"I don't think of it that way."

"You may this time. Tonight it's a girl. She's in trouble and she needs a place to stay; but more than that, she needs a woman who can understand."

"Do I know her?"

"Judy Polsen."

"The hill girl. I've seen her in town."

"Her father whipped her tonight and drove her out. I don't think from what Shorham said that she's badly hurt, at least, not physically; but there's something more." He went on to tell about Jet Cosgrave and the meeting in Salt Canyon.

She said once, "Whipped her," and then was silent, giving him her steady attention yet never missing the rhythm of her stitches. When he finished she said: "Bring her here, Sam. Why didn't you bring her at once?"

He said: "I should have known, but it doesn't seem quite fair. It's none of your concern and—"

"But it is," she said. "We all live in the world, Sam. We couldn't ignore it if we would, and I for one wouldn't. Bring her here, and we'll straighten this out somehow."

Judy came unwillingly. Her trust in women was even less than her trust in men, but despite her reserve she found herself telling the whole story to Nan Ireland before she had been in the house an hour.

Nan was businesslike. She peeled off the bloodstained

shirt without comment, although the crossed welts on the girl's back made her wince. Judy was stoical, uttering no sound, but her eyes thanked Nan Ireland when she had finished.

"And now," said the dressmaker, "you need a rest."

"I've got to work." The girl's eyes were on the silk which still draped the cutting table. "I've got to work and I've got to learn things. It never seemed to matter much before, but now it's important."

Nan Ireland watched her sitting beneath the lamp, her young body bared to the waist, her breasts round and firm and proud.

" I want dresses. I want him to be proud of me. I don't want to be hill trash."

It was the first mention she had made of Cosgrave, and the woman did not press her; but to Judy the day had been a milestone, changing her thoughts and purposes and her hopes. She found that she had to talk to someone, to share this new thing which threatened to burst inside of her.

The woman's eyes were soft with understanding. "You think you love him, don't you?"

"Think?" Judy looked at her. "Think? It's—it's something I can't understand; the way I feel, the way I want to live, the—" She was at a loss for words.

She's beautiful, Nan Ireland thought. If any man could see her at this moment, he'd never in the world let her go. But she's so defenseless. She has no experience, no measuring stick. To her this is something brand-new. It's never happened to anyone else in the world. I wonder what Jet Cosgrave is like. If he's like his uncle, he'd never understand. He'd take her trust and break her belief and never even know.

Aloud she murmured: "I know how you feel. You can't wait until you see him again. You think every minute that passes is something golden forever lost. But believe me, you're young. You've still got a lot of time for happiness. Don't rush at it blindly. Get your feet under you."

The girl looked at her, and Nan read her thoughts.

"Your'e wondering how I know," she said. "You're thinking I'm plain and tired and middle-aged."

"No," said Judy. "No."

"And you think me an old maid, perhaps. I'm not that. I was married when I wasn't quite your age, and I was just as eager." Nan sighed. "But that's enough talk for one night; tomorrow we'll find something for you to wear and decide what to do with you."

"I want to work," said Judy. "I want to find out how people live."

Nan Ireland considered her. "Work never hurt anyone. I'll see Martha Appley in the morning. With these fixings for the Major's wedding they can probably use an extra girl at the hotel. It isn't every hotel I'd want you to work in, certainly not in Jim Banner's place; but Martha is different: she allows for no foolishness at the Colton House. But we'll have to fix you up a dress. Martha wouldn't stand for a waitress in pants. She'd never be able to hold up her head in Sunday church. Come on, I'll show you where to sleep."

11

Jet Cosgrave slept more soundly than Judy did that night. He did not hear the horse guard slip into the cabin and rouse Rankin, nor did he hear Rankin return to his blankets after his meeting with Prince.

In the morning he put three men to work sinking poles for a holding fence so that the cattle which they combed from the brush could be rebranded and held without drifting. The fence was not a thing of beauty, but it would serve. The rest of the crew labored to build a branding chute, and Jet worked with them.

At eleven Curly pulled into the yard. He had driven to Lone Star for supplies, and his wagon was piled high with flour, sacked beans, blankets, and molasses. The crew unloaded the wagon, carrying the plunder to the cookshack, and Jet looked around him with growing satisfaction. Already the layout was shaping up, and they had been in the valley only a little over twenty-four hours. The only thing that bothered him was Rankin's attitude. The man had accepted orders all morning without objection, but he was unusually quiet and thoughtful, as if he had something on his mind.

They were at lunch, eating outdoors because there was no table large enough inside, when Sam's boy rode up. He looked very small perched on the high horse, and he was nervous until he spotted Cosgrave. Then his slow, friendly grin spread across his face.

"Sam wants you," he said without climbing down.

Cosgrave rose, ordered a man to turn the boy's horse into the corral, and told Curly to fill an extra plate. "What's Sam want, Steve?"

The boy was already eating, his mouth full. "Sam didn't say. He just wants you to ride in."

Cosgrave saw Rankin watching him with an expression he did not understand. It was almost as if his trail boss had been waiting for something like this to happen, as if he were eager for Cosgrave to leave. But that was absurd. He thought: I'm getting spooky. I shouldn't develop nerves now. I've got other things to think about, other things on my mind.

He waited until the boy had finished, then saddled his own horse and caught up a fresh mount for Steve.

"You tired?"

"Hell," said the boy, "I never get tired."

Cosgrave looked at him sharply and Steve's face reddened. "I never say 'hell' in front of the ladies," was the way he worded his apology. Cosgrave concealed his smile as he swung his horse down the valley trail with Steve riding at his heels. Had he looked back he would have seen Rankin grinning broadly as the big trail boss watched them go.

In fact they were hardly out of hearing when Rankin addressed the crew. "How many steers do you think we can comb out of the brush this afternoon?"

When they looked at him in surprise, he quickly outlined Prince's proposition. He expected no objections. Most of these men were outlaws, recruited by him. A few murmured protests, and he pulled the bill of sale from his pocket, showing them Prince's signature.

"Why should we stay here and fight?" he demanded. "We can gather a herd before young Cosgrave gets back from town, drive them through the pass and sell them on the reservation. Let's get moving." Motioning to one man to follow, he rose and moved out of hearing distance of the crew.

"Don't tell the others," he warned, "but get a horse. Ride to the Circle C. Tell Cal Prince that I said young Cosgrave is headed for town and to take care of him."

The man gave him a tight-lipped, understanding smile, and Rankin turned back to the grouped men. "The rest of you start gathering the herd; we want to be away from here by daylight."

They hesitated, and the cook looked sullen; but Rankin took no notice, leading the way to the corral.

By the time they were mounted, Jet and the boy had reached the lower end of the valley, dropping from sight. It was warm, and Jet slowed the pace, turning in his saddle to ask, "Haven't you any idea what Sam wants?"

Steve was careful with his answer. Naturally close-mouthed, he preferred to let the printer do the talking.

"Sam just said it was important you should ride in."

Jet Cosgrave did not know whether to be amused or not. He hated to waste the time riding to town, but it was obvious that he wasn't going to get any more information from the boy. He gave up questioning and rode forward in silence, holding a steady gait that ate up the miles without tiring the mounts. Whatever Sam's reason for sending for him, it must be important for the printer to start the red-headed boy on such a long ride alone.

Steve rode easily, however, showing no sign that he had been in the saddle since before dawn, and he seemed to take a real joy in the experience; but he was always watchful, as if constantly on guard. Jet noted this approvingly. The kid will make a hand, he thought, if Sam doesn't spoil him with too much learning.

Aloud he asked, "Did you run into anyone on the trail?"

Steve turned his head. "I made certain not to," he grinned. "People you meet ask questions sometimes."

Cosgrave nodded. They came to the mouth of the canyon and bore left, following the ragged line of the hills in a wide detour, for the Circle C lay directly on the main trail to town. The range was heavily stocked, for as the summer heat increased the Circle C had drifted their cattle farther and farther toward the green, lush meadows of the Larkspurs. Cosgrave smiled quietly. The cows he wanted had been practically dumped in his lap. Twice they saw riders far off on the horizon, and both times they turned into the hills, waiting until they were certain they had not been observed.

Night found them still five miles from Colton, but with its sheltering dusk they increased their pace, cutting now across the flatter plain. They circled the town, coming in from the other end, and pulled their horses up behind Allen's house. Here Jet stepped from the saddle. The boy caught his rein and led his horse through a maze of alleys toward the livery.

Sam Allen was alone, lounging before the wood range of the kitchen, his legs covered with a protective white apron. Cosgrave's approach was so quiet that Allen did not know he was there until he thrust open the rear door and stood pretending to admire the printer.

"Sam," he said, stepping forward enough to close the door. "You look sweet. If you could only cook, I'd marry you."

"Save your humor," the printer told him sourly. "You may need it before you get out of town."

"What's happened? Why did you send Steve for me? What's the Major done now?"

"It isn't the Major," said Sam. "Come on and eat. I never kill a man on an empty stomach."

Jet looked at him sharply, but the printer was busy at the stove. Turning to the washbasin, Cosgrave removed the trail dust from his face and hands and seated himself on one of the three-legged stools. The readheaded boy had not returned; this in itself was disquieting, but Allen did not appear to notice. Jet watched him, his mystification growing. It wasn't like the printer to be roundabout. He never hedged a point, even in print, which was one reason why he sometimes found himself at odds with the town authorities.

"Look." Jet Cosgrave laid his fork aside. "If this is a game I'm ready to have my laugh and start back. You send Steve clear into the Larkspur hills and I come tearing down, half kill a horse, and you sit there like a wooden Indian, as if you had nothing on your mind but food."

"I've got aplenty," Allen told him, "but like I said, it's against my principles to kill a man on an empty stomach."

"Meaning me?"

"Meaning you."

Cosgrave said: "Shoot ahead, friend. I've got a tough crew at the ranch, and I don't feel easy leaving them too much alone. I've got things on my mind."

"What things?" said Allen.

Jet looked at him. "I don't get it, Sam. You're not the same. You're looking at me like a judge. Is it bothering you that I'm going after the Major?"

"It isn't," said Allen promptly. "The Major can take care of himself. Judy can't."

"Judy?" Cosgrave started to lift a hand toward his shirt pocket where his tobacco lay, then let it fall. "You mean Judy Polsen? What's the matter with her?"

"You didn't know she'd left home?"

"Left home? Look, Sam, stop the riddles. Tell me what you're trying to say, straight out."

"Are you in love with her?" Allen asked. "Do you mean to marry her?"

"Marry her? Are you crazy, Sam?"

"I was afraid of this." Sam Allen's mouth was a tight line.

"Hey, wait a minute." Jet was too surprised to think clearly. "What's this all about?"

Allen told him then, using short sentences and expressive words. "I'm not entirely blaming you, Jet. Any man might do the same. The hell of it is, Judy isn't an ordinary woman. You've got to remember that she raised herself without much help from that old wart-hog of a father. Her brothers are Indians. The old man whipped her."

Cosgrave kicked the stool from under him and stood above the printer. "Whipped her?"

"I wish you could have seen her last night when I took her to Nan Ireland's."

Cosgrave's hand shook as he rubbed it through his hair. "I'll have to do something about that."

"That's right," said Allen steadily. "You're the only one who can do anything. You'll marry her. You kissed her, and she'll never believe that you'd kiss her unless you loved her, meant her to be your wife."

Jet's stare widened on the man. "She has an odd way of showing her affection. Did she tell you she put a bullet through my hat?"

"She told Nan Ireland. She was panicky at the thought that she might have hit you. I don't know how many women you've known or been interested in—the girl on the train, for instance."

Cosgrave started to laugh, then sobered. He had been attracted by the girl on the train. There was no denying it.

The printer went on, not noticing his changed expression. "In thinking of Judy you can't judge her by other women. The only ideas she has are ones she's dug up for herself. She's honest. She couldn't flirt with a man if she tried. She thinks you love her, otherwise why did you kiss her? You're going to marry her, Jet; and if you give her a rough time, you'll have to answer to me."

Cosgrave said: "You're crazy, Sam. A man can't marry a girl he kissed on impulse."

"She'd never understand that," Allen said. "She's lost what little she had in the way of a home because of you. If you turn her down, it will break her all up, turn her God knows which way. I'm not going to let that happen. You're going to marry her and you're going to pretend to love her. You'll pretend so well that she'll never know the difference."

Cosgrave stared at him. "I've always suspected you were a romanticist. But face facts. I'm in a war; I've grabbed the line camp and brought in a tough crew. The law will be against me—what law this county has. If the Major's men brought me in, the marshal would do his best to hang me. Is that the kind of a husband you want for Judy?"

"Well, no, but—"

"There aren't any buts. Her brothers will be on my trail whether I marry her or not. They'll hunt me down if they can, and they probably can. And suppose I married her. What could we do? I couldn't take her to Newmark Valley.

I wouldn't trust any woman to that bunch of wolves, even if she could handle a rifle twice as well as Judy can. That crew of mine would shoot me down as quick as the Major, if it served their purpose."

"You could go away," said Allen.

Cosgrave stared at him. "Go away? After all my planning, after the years I've waited for this chance? I'm afraid you don't know me, Sam. I wouldn't give up fighting the Major for a thousand women."

"You should have thought of that before you kissed her."

"Quit it," said Cosgrave, and swung away from the table. "If a man stopped to think before every kiss, half the trouble in this world would be avoided. This is the damnedest thing I ever heard of. You're trying to help the girl. Will it help her to be married to me when I dance at the end of a Circle C rope? Or fall in the brush with her brother's bullet in my back? Use your head, Sam. Even if you loved her, you'd never marry her in my spot."

"I wouldn't have kissed her in the first place."

Cosgrave looked back at him slowly and said in a different voice: "I don't believe you would. You were born to be a monk, Sam. I used to watch you before I went away and wonder then. I've known for years that you've eaten your heart out for Nan Ireland."

"Shut up."

"No. You can tell me what to do, so there's no reason why I shouldn't return the compliment. For years you've stood back because of that peg leg. Forget it. Go up there like a man and tell her what's in your heart. She's known it ever since I can remember, but she's never found a way to make you speak."

Allen's face whitened. "You're crazy."

"Granted," said Jet. "Anyone with the name Cosgrave is crazy. But I'm sane on this. Why don't you stop worrying about other people and think about yourself and Nan?" He swung toward the door, and his hand was on the latch when Allen's voice stopped him.

"Where are you going?"

"Up to Nan Ireland's to try to make Judy understand what a heel I am."

"Jet, don't go up there with that attitude. If that's the way you feel, don't go near the girl at all."

"Look," said Cosgrave, purposely rude. "You keep out of my life and I'll keep out of yours." He turned into the darkness, slamming the door behind him.

As he strode along he wondered what he could say to the girl, and muttered under his breath. What the devil had been the matter with him? He must have been crazy to have kissed her. If he had even stopped to think, he'd have realized that the worst thing he could do was to get involved with the Polsens. And now she had left home because of him. He swore at himself. Women. Women should be beautiful and decorative—and keep out of a man's way. They should be ladies, like the girl on the train, not half-civilized children who wore britches and could shoot a man out of the saddle. He grinned in spite of himself at the remembrance of the way she had held the Circle C men under her rifle. Lucky for him that she'd been able to use a gun—but marry her! When he married, he wanted a lady. He was like the Major in this: he wanted a lady to decorate his house.

He moved along the alley so wrapped in his thoughts that he was careless. It was the one thing his training should have prevented. His mind should have been on the town, on the shadows and the danger; not on Allen's words, not on the two girls, so utterly different in background and upbringing and appearance.

"Captain," said the long-haired Bert. "You should be more watchful."

They were around him suddenly, drifting out of the narrow passages between the store buildings on both sides of the alley. He couldn't be certain how many there were, five or six, or more. Bert stood directly before him, showing faintly in the dim penumbra of light from a high window. One moment he had been alone in the dark, empty alley. Now it was filled with men.

This was the second time they had ambushed him, and

he knew that he deserved to die. He knew that he should curse himself for his inattention, but the rage he had felt at being trapped on the first night was not there. He was washed now by a coldness that left every sense alert. If they killed him, here in the dust, the Major would win. He would rally his crew and drive Rankin and the men from the hills, or kill them on the wooded mountain slopes.

Small loss, he thought; no one would regret his passing. Judy might, but then Judy had built up a picture of him in her mind that had little to do with reality. He wished for an instant that she were here with the rifle she handled so readily. It was possible that she might take it on herself to hunt down these men. The Polsens were as good haters as the Cosgraves were. . . .

He heard the Kid's jeering voice. "Captain, you shouldn't have let that newspaper kid take your horse to the livery. Prince is behind you, Captain, with a scattergun. This time you don't get away."

He knew it was no bluff. They had him on the hip, and there was no reason to expect chivalry from the Circle C.

"Start shooting," he said.

Prince laughed, and his gravelly voice was close to Cosgrave's shoulder. "We could have shot you without talking, but the Major wants no rough stuff until after the wedding. It's a break you don't deserve, Cosgrave. We'll turn you in to the marshal for murder. If the court doesn't handle you, we will, later. Get his gun, Kid."

Bert moved in close, tense as a stalking panther, keeping a little to one side so he could reach the holstered gun. He slipped it free, flipped it to one of the men, and then struck Cosgrave's face, raking his knuckles hard against the mouth.

"You're not going to get off too easy, Captain. You laid a hand on me, and I don't like that." He struck again, this time a solid blow that jerked Jet's head back and jarred his senses.

Cosgrave's movement was purely instinctive. His arms shot out, catching Bert's narrower shoulders and wrapping about them, dragging the man against his face until his nostrils were filled with the sweat smell from the long greasy hair. Then he got a boot heel behind Bert's legs and heaved against him, crashing them both to the thick dust cushion of the alley floor.

He heard the slighter man cry out, startled and struggling. He heard the jumbled curses of the crew and Prince's strident orders to pull them apart. He rolled now toward the building line and came half to his feet as Bert broke his hold. A heavy boot caught him squarely in the ribs, sending a hot quick pain racing through his side. By luck he caught the swinging boot and upset the man. A shotgun fell to the dirt at his side, and he knew then that the kicker had been Prince. He seized the gun blindly, brought it half up and discharged both barrels, the mule kick of the explosion tearing the weapon from his fingers.

Someone cried out in shock and pain. He found himself against a store wall and dragged himself upright as the barrel of a revolver clipped down along the side of his head, tearing at his ear. He shook his head, trying to dispel the confusing blur. A body lunged in and he struck heavily, catching the man full in the stomach with an underhand blow. Air belched from the man's mouth and he hung for an instant limply across Cosgrave's fists and then collapsed moaning.

Their very numbers made it hard for them. The light was so uncertain that it was hard to separate friend from foe, but all the while he heard Bert's high-pitched yelling: "Let me have him. Let me have him." He surged away from the wall, carrying with him two men who had rushed in battering at his face. He stumbled and almost fell as his knees hit the rising Prince. He knocked the man aside. Something was running down into his eyes. He guessed that it was blood but had no time to give it further thought, for Prince grabbed him by the legs. He kicked free, feeling his boot toe sink into the man's face but not hearing the foreman's groan.

Then Bert closed with him again, flailing with hard fists, using his elbows and his knees. Cosgrave brought up his own knee and hit the Kid in the groin; he knew that he was hurt by the way he sagged. A gun swung from behind caught the crown of Jet's head in a glancing blow and he staggered, almost going down. He saw the flash of Bert's long knife, saw the man crouch; and he knew that there lay a greater danger than any other. As the lithe man charged, he seized the knife wrist, pivoted on his boot heels, and tried to heave Bert over his head. He failed. He simply did not have enough left. Instead they fell together, with the knife hand under Cosgrave, the sharp point scraping across his stomach.

He did not know how deep the cut was and had no time to care. Someone was on his back, trying to haul him free, and he rolled, bending the wrist below him, tearing the knife from Bert's grasping fingers, and taking it with him. He found the strength to rise to one knee, and in that second Bert jumped, as blind as Cosgrave and as past caring. Their bodies came together with a shock and sprawled, writhing. Cosgrave's arm was twisted under Bert's body, but he did not know for the instant that the knife was upright and that the gunman had impaled himself on it. He did not know until he tried to drag the knife free and found it caught too solidly for his strength. Then he let it go and rolled away. This time Bert made no move to follow, lying crumpled where Cosgrave left him.

In his roll Jet's arm hit the shotgun and he snagged it to him, catching it by the barrels. Staggering up, he used the heavy stock as a club. His attackers were not so eager now, but Prince charged in and got the full swing of the gun across his shoulders and fell backward. In the little swirl of silence Cosgrave felt behind him for the steadying wall. It wasn't there. For an instant the knowledge failed to register, then he realized that he stood before the crack between two building walls, and stepped back into the unexpected shelter.

It was only two feet wide, and he groped along it in almost total darkness, hearing the renewed shouts in the alley at his back. He let the gun go and used both hands to feel the walls. It would be only moments before they discovered him, and he pushed ahead desperately, the sound of his fumbling covered by the raucous noises of the Circle C hands. The way to the street ahead was blocked by a board bulkhead that extended upward to the eaves of the buildings on either side. He knew that he could not have climbed it even if he had been at full strength.

His mind was not clear. Waves of nausea swept up through his aching body, almost blacking out his consciousness. Even the pain from his hurts was dulled. He knew that his right arm was nearly useless, that his head ached sharply, that his tortured lungs fought for the air he needed.

And then he found the window. His stretching fingers outlined the panes, carrying the slow message to his brain. He stood still, fearing that the sound of his retching would bring them into the passageway after him. He tried the window but it seemed to be locked, and he almost gave up and let his big body settle to the ground. He dared not break the glass, for the noise would bring them about him like angry hornets. He pushed upward on the top edge of the lower sash, and though he thought it was hopeless he pushed again. This time the stubborn window gave, the old sash squealing in protest. He thought that they must have heard it, that everyone in Colton must have heard it, but he did not stop. The crack at the bottom was wide enough to get his fingers under. He heaved, feeling the muscles in his neck cord with the effort, and the window rose, not wide, but enough for him to work his shoulders through and fall headforemost into the storeroom beyond. He somersaulted to the board floor, and for a full minute he had not the strength to rise; then, painfully, he dragged himself erect and turned, using his good hand to shut the window.

The noise in the alley was fainter now, its volume dampened by the intervening walls. But he could still hear them calling to each other, still hear Prince's bellowed curses as he directed the man hunt.

"He can't get far," the foreman was shouting. "Spread out. The Major will skin us all if he gets away. Search every damn' building in the block; and don't forget, he killed the Kid."

12

The knowledge that Bert was dead brought no pleasure, no sense of accomplishment. He had not even hated the long-haired boy. Even when Bert had struck him he had known no hatred, and now he only wanted to get away.

He turned into the darkened store, feeling his way forward. There was an odor of freshly ground coffee, the smell of spice and of new hemp rope. This would be Saddler's General Merchandise Establishment, and with that recognition Cosgrave continued his search until he found the ladderlike stairs to the little balcony office above.

Once in the office he could see the shadowy shape of the bookkeeper's high desk and the dark outline of the old safe in the faint light that seeped through the skylight. He paused, giddy and panting, and stared around for some place to hide. The skylight attracted him. He stared at it for a long moment, then climbed heavily upon the crest of the rolltop desk. Finding that he could reach the frame easily, he fumbled for the catch. It was stuck, but he managed to work it loose after a dozen tries. When he got his hands over the edge of the opening, his right arm felt dead. He wondered if he could lift himself. Twice he failed, but on the third attempt he wedged one of his boot heels against the side and with this purchase managed to half climb, half walk up the wall, rolling out belly flat upon the roof. He twisted away from the glassed hole and slid the cover back into place. He could not fasten the latch because it was on the inside, but he wasted only a moment's worry on this.

Remotely above him arched the night sky. There was no moon, but the rash of stars gave enough light to show the flat roof in fair detail. It was metal, and he went across it on hands and knees knowing that he would not thus be as apt to give away his position to the searching men. He reached the rear coping and peeped over cautiously. He had lost his hat, and he was careful not to show his head enough to be silhouetted against the lighter sky.

They had lighted a lantern below him and the men were spread out along the alley. Prince stood beside Bert's body, blocky and heavy in the yellow light, bawling his orders. The crew had been joined by other men, perhaps from the marshal's office, for there were at least a dozen of them now. As Cosgrave listened, they set their search with care, ringing the block, with a crew of searchers to go through each building.

"Don't miss a single corner," Prince warned. "I want that killer and I want him tonight. A hundred dollars in gold to the man who brings him in or shows me where his body is."

Cosgrave's heart sank. A hundred dollars was three months' pay. It would be a windfall to any saddle tramp. As soon as the news of the man hunt spread, every saloon and gambling hall would be empty. In place of the present dozen there would be a hundred men, all bent on his destruction. Any chance of escape was almost hopelessly thin. Already they were posting guards at the side streets so that he could not hope to get off the block. They'd search the stores and warehouses, and then someone would think of the roofs. It occurred to him to give himself up now. He was so very tired and his head ached so badly that it did not seem to matter whether he was taken now or an hour from now. But something in him, some instinct deeper than conscious thought, held him back and made him turn and crawl across the roof.

The next building had been built against the general store, with only a fire wall of brick between them. He sprawled across it and found himself on another metal roof, and so progressed for almost the full length of the block. Twice he had to jump intervening spaces. Once he slipped, nearly falling to the earth below, but he saved himself by throwing his full weight forward, coming face down on the rough weathered corrugations of the next roof. He lay gasping, his face masked with a heavy sweat that felt cold and sticky in the night wind. Then he crawled on until he came to the wall of the Colton House.

The hotel was two-storied, while the other buildings in the block had but a single floor. He stopped, staring at the windows ranged along the wall facing him. Only two of them showed light, and only one was partly open. A good three feet yawned between the sill of the open window and the edge of the roof on which he crouched. He hesitated, trying to peer into the room; but beyond the open sash the heavy curtains were so drawn that, while light showed out, he could not see into the room.

He drew a deep breath and came to his feet, turning for an instant to look backward across the roofs. The skylight of Saddler's store suddenly showed light, and this decided him. They were searching the store; and bleeding as he was, he had probably left some marks of his passage. If they saw the signs on the side of the skylight, it would lead them to the roof. He waited no longer but leaned across, the fingers of his left hand catching the edge of the raised sash, and stepped over to the stone sill. He stood there for an instant, his feet firm but his body leaning out over nothingness, and a wave of nausea almost loosened his grip and let him fall backward. Then he went into the room feet first, his knees knocking the curtains away for the passage of his body. He missed his footing, his boot heels hooking up the edge of a small throw rug and skidding with it so that he dropped against the window. His shoulder blades hit the sharp inside sill and he slid down, seated against the wall, blinded by the curtains. Dully he heard a startled gasp, then his good hand pushed the curtain aside and he found himself looking upward into the astonished eyes of the girl from the train.

For an instant he thought his aching mind had given way and that he was dreaming, then he tried to sit up but bumped his head against the sill. The bump seemed to bring him to. It gave him enough sense to reach up and pull down the sash. As he did so he saw men emerging from the distant skylight. Quickly he let the curtain fall back into place, swinging around on his knees. Alice Austin had not moved but was still staring at him.

He said hoarsely, "Lock the door, ma'am, unless you want to see me murdered on your floor."

She obeyed automatically, backing to the door and twisting the key without taking her eyes from his battered face. "You're hurt."

"Ma'am," he asid, "you don't know the half of it." He struggled upright, staggering as he crossed to the wash-stand. There he picked up the pitcher as if it weighed a thousand pounds and tried to drink from it, spilling water over himself in a splashing cascade.

"Here." Alice Austin stepped quickly forward. "Let me." She took the pitcher from his grasp, trying to steady it, and to her horror saw his legs give under him and watched him crumple to the floor at her feet.

Never in her twenty-two years had she seen a man who had been in a fight; and as she looked down at his bloody face, at the cut across his forehead, the left eye almost closed, it seemed to her that he must be dead. She shivered. Her natural reaction was to step away from him, but she forced herself to replace the pitcher in the bowl and bend down.

He had fallen on his side, his big body folded a little, his head pillowed on one arm like that of a small boy asleep. She tried to lift him but only succeeded in straightening his body. In so doing she found the front of his shirt cut through and the deep scratch which the knife point had made across his stomach. Now she was certain that he was dead and she turned away, only to hear his muttered protest: "Don't tell the Major I'm here, ma'am. Don't tell the Major."

She turned back. The Major. She had heard enough casual gossip to know that the Major's nephew had returned and that there was some quarrel about the ranch; but it shocked her to realize that this broken man owed his condition to his uncle, to the man she had come west to marry. The certain knowledge sickened her. Then Cosgrave groaned, and she forgot her own mental turmoil in the realization that something had to be done for him.

Hearing a noise beyond the window, she crossed, parted the curtains an inch, and stared out. Men were clustered on the roof of the next building, studying the hotel wall. She pulled the curtains quickly together, knowing that these dark shadows must be hunting the beaten man who lay behind her.

But what to do? To whom should she appeal? Her first thought was of the hotel people. Martha Appley, the owner's wife, was big and competent and friendly. The trouble was that she was too friendly with the Major. There was no one, not a soul whom Alice Austin felt that she could trust, and yet she obviously had to have help. The man certainly needed a doctor. She walked back and looked down at him. His physical resemblance to the Major, despite the brutal marks, was plain. She wondered why she had failed to see it on the train. But then she had been carefully avoiding men, avoiding the efforts of the fat salesman to talk to her—the salesman, that was it! She had seen him that afternoon as she drove along the street with the banker's wife. He'd been sitting in one of the chairs under the wooden awning of the Banner House, where he was probably staying. He had seemed friendly to Jet Cosgrave on the train. If she could get to him.

She turned toward the door, still having sufficient presence of mind to pick up her bonnet as she passed the chair. Slipping out, she locked the door behind her.

Going down the stairs she found the lobby in an air of mild excitement. A big man in dust-covered clothes, with a jagged tear across the shoulder of his gray shirt, was talking to Tom Appley. She recognized him as the man named Prince who had met her at the station and had introduced himself as the Major's foreman. Fear closed about her heart, gripping it into a small tight ball that climbed upward into her throat until she felt that it would stifle her.

Neither man turned to look at her, but as she passed behind Prince and hurried to the door she heard him say in a dangerous voice: "I'm going to search your rooms, Tom. I tell you he was on that roof. He had to come through this hotel."

"Bring the marshal if you want to do any searching." Appley was quietly stubborn.

"But's he's a murderer," said Prince. "He knifed the Kid in the alley."

"Bring the marshal." Appley's tone had not changed.

"The Major won't like this." Prince's words were a threat.

"Bring the marshal. The Major doesn't run this hotel."

Prince swore and came away from the desk, brushing by Alice Austin without noticing her and saying to a man beside the door: "Watch the stairs, Sawyer. Don't let him out. I'll get the marshal like the old fool wants." He disappeared into the night, and Alice Austin went after him.

She had to hurry. If they meant to search the hotel, she had to be back in her room, to stop them somehow. She did not try to analyze her actions, or try to understand why she was doing this for a man who had been publicly proclaimed a murderer. She knew only that she must hurry. She almost dashed down Linden, turning into Parker Alley without realizing that she was traveling a street no decent woman ever entered if she could avoid it.

Ordinarily the alley would have been thronged, but now its visitors had been siphoned off by the excitement of the man hunt, and its length was nearly deserted. A drunken rider staggered out of Mable Hayes's, called to her, and tried to catch her arm, but she ran on, gaining the bright lightness of Fremont and turning toward the Banner House.

George Pitman sat in one of the hotel's cane-bottomed chairs, his bulk flowing over the arms, enjoying the coolness which was so refreshing after the heat of the day. He shared his vantage point with two other salesmen who from bitter experience knew the temper of the local celebrants and kept out of the saloons. All three saw the girl as she hurried toward them, watching her speculatively, after the manner of their kind. But Pitman did not recognize her until she had almost reached them.

She stopped then and said in a hurried undertone: "I was with you on the train, remember? Please, I need help."

She turned away quickly, not waiting for his answer, and started back the way she had come.

Pitman hesitated. His slow mind was caught by the unexpectedness of her appeal, but caution warned him not to follow her. The expressive whistle of one of his fellows was what decided him. He lifted his bulk from the chair and hurried after her, noting that she had halted a dozen feet away.

"Miss, what is it? I—"

"The young fellow on the train." She said it in a tense whisper. "The one who helped you carry my things. He's hurt, in my room, and men are hunting him. I need your help."

Pitman knew who she was. He'd heard the gossip from the merchants. She was to marry this mysterious Major, the Major who was both the boy's uncle and his enemy. It made no sense, and Pitman was one who liked things to make sense. "Wait—"

"No time," she said. "They're going to search the Colton House, my room. I've got to be there to stop them. It's No. 8. Come as fast as you can." Then she turned and fled.

The fat man followed. All the way through Parker Alley he told himself how foolish this move was. He knew that he was not a fighting man. He knew also, and had known for years, that he was a coward; the temptation to turn back was very strong. Then he thought of Jet Cosgrave, alone and friendless in a hostile town. The big cowboy had been pleasant on the train, pleasant and friendly, and George Pitman appreciated friendship. He hurried on, puffing as he went, noting the small knots of men gathered along the street, the intent groups going in and out of buildings, following their search with deadly precision. There was a grimness about the town which had not been there an hour before. Citizens who had nothing against Jet Cosgrave, who knew no loyalty to the Major or the Circle C, had joined the hunt, caught up in the psychology of the mob which in a few short seconds can change law-abiding men into ruthless, crazy killers.

George Pitman sweated as he passed each armed group, acutely aware of what might happen to him if it were learned that he had gone to young Cosgrave's aid. But he did not turn back. He reached the Colton House, entered and climbed the stairs, feeling Sawyer's hard eyes against his back as the Circle C man watched his ascent from the vantage place beside the entrance.

13

Back in her room Alice
Austin shut the door hastily and turned the key in the lock.
The man on the floor had not moved; and apparently the
marshal had not arrived, for the search of the hotel had
not yet begun.

She stood weakly, her back to the door, trying to still her
labored breathing. Everything that had happened since she
had reached this town was unreal, unbelievable. In Chicago the idea of marrying the Major had seemed feasible. She
had not been in love with him, but she had honored him as
a business associate of her father. At her father's death,
when it was discovered that the family resources had
shrunk almost to nothingness, it was the Major who hurried east to salvage what little he could for her. Despite her
inexperience she had an honesty of self-appraisal which
made her realize her own limitations and her utter inability
to handle her own affairs. When the Major offered marriage, she turned quickly to him, grateful for his strength.
She did not pretend to love him and he had not demanded
that she should. She guessed shrewdly that he admired her,
that it would feed his ego to have a pretty woman for a wife,
and that as long as she did not disgrace him he would ask
for little else.

But could she marry him now? Three days in this hotel
had shown her a roughness in this country that she had not
anticipated. A man lay bleeding on the floor, the nephew
of her future husband, beat down by Circle C hands. She
shuddered, then turned quickly as there was a light rap at
the door.

"Who is it?"

"George Pitman."

She realized then that she had not known his name, and the thought brought a wave of hysteria which she fought down with difficulty. She let him in and he stood wheezing from his hurried trip, wiping the sweat from his bulging neck and staring down at Cosgrave.

"My," he said, and there was deep pity in his tone, "I've seen men beat up, but never like this." He got down on his knees and examined Cosgrave.

"Friend," he said, speaking to the unconscious man. "I tried to warn you to leave this town, but your kind doesn't take warning. You're so very confident of your own strength, of your own ability. You should know fear, as I have. It would make you more sensible."

The girl's voice cut across his words with quick impatience. "Do something."

The fat man looked up at her, his eyes mild. "I'm not a doctor, ma'am."

She caught herself, realizing the injustice of her tone. "I'm sorry." She had been so certain that once she got help everything would be all right. Previously she had always been able to shift responsibility. Never before had she been forced to make decisions; but the fat man was more uncertain than she, and unconsciously she took command. "Help me lift him to the bed."

Together they raised Cosgrave's battered body, Pitman revealing surprising strength under his layers of flesh. They stripped off his coat and poured water into the bowl. With the girl holding it, Pitman washed away the blood.

"Shouldn't he have a doctor?"

The fat man glanced at her. "No chance. A doctor seen entering the hotel would be a dead giveaway."

She had known this but had not wanted to make the decision alone. "But maybe he'll die."

"He'll die if they find him." Pitman sounded unhappy. "He'll wind up at the end of a rope."

She shivered. There seemed to be no law here, none except that which men made themselves, hunting each other down as if they were predatory animals. She looked again at the man on the bed, noting his resemblance to the man she had come west to marry, and thought: They're the same, and except for the difference in age it might be the Major lying there. She bit her lip, wondering what her re-action would have been, and turned away shuddering.

The fat man misunderstood and tried to reassure her. "This cowboy is tough. This isn't his first fight. Look at the scars."

"I—you think he's going to die?"

"I don't know." Pitman was covering Cosgrave with a blanket. "I don't think so. It's wonderful what men can stand. The Lord gave us good bodies, and we abuse them." He looked down regretfully at his big stomach, then looked at the girl. "I'm wondering why you do this. I'd heard that you are on the other side."

She was startled. "Heard, from whom?"

"A salesman picks up gossip." He was embarrassed.

"Of course," she said. "Of course . . . this terrible town. A man's life isn't safe here. I wonder you aren't afraid to stay."

He shrugged. "I am." He sighed. "Every time I start a trip I wonder if I'll come back, but a man has a job. I've been here three days. I'll have to stay a couple more. A man I have to sell to is out of town, I—" He broke off as heavy boots tramped up the stairs and Prince's dominating tone reached them clearly.

"Start at the front, Marshal. Search every room. I don't think he's armed but have your guns ready. All right, Ap-pley, open the doors."

The girl turned, pressing the back of her hand tightly across her mouth. The fat man knew his own fear. If he were found here, it would be something that the Major would not forgive or forget. He stood rooted to the spot, but after the first sharp surprise the girl moved quickly, pulling the blanket up to conceal Cosgrave's head.

"Blow out the light." The words were a whisper.

George Pitman obeyed, then stepped toward the corner so that the opening door would partly conceal him. Desper-ately he wished that he had a gun, although he knew that there were half a dozen men in the hall and that there was no escape. Then he heard a fumbling in the darkness and the soft swish of silk as it was dropped across the chair. Cold sweat beaded his forehead. The girl was undressing. If they broke into the room now and found him here, with the Major's bride . . . They wouldn't dare, and yet the men had been drinking. . . . He listened to their noisy approach, his fat knees so weak that they would scarcely hold his weight, and wished that he was safe in Kansas City, safe under the blankets with his colorless wife. They were in the next room, and the walls were so thin that he was certain they could hear his taut breathing. They returned to the hall and he heard the hotel owner protesting.

"That room belongs to Miss Austin. The Major won't want her disturbed." His tone grew heavy with sarcasm. "You don't expect to find Jet hiding under *her* bed, do you?"

Prince said hoarsely: "Maybe she isn't there. Maybe Jet crawled through her window. Open it up."

Instead Appley knocked, his knuckles rapping hollowly on the panel. The girl said steadily, in a low voice: "What is it? Who's there?"

"It's me." Tom Appley had no liking for his role. "We're looking for a murderer, miss. We'd like to search your room."

"Search my room?" She managed to get surprise and indignation into her tone. "Have you gone insane? I've retired."

There was a muttered conference in the hall and at that instant Jet Cosgrave groaned. Almost paralyzed, the fat man eased across, slid his big hand under the blanket, and pressed his fingers against Cosgrave's lips. The girl kept her head. Nothing of her rising panic showed as she raised her voice to mask any sound.

"You certainly aren't daring to suggest that I have anyone in here with me? If you don't stop this disturbance at once, I'll complain to Major Cosgrave in the morning."

"She's right," the marshal said. "She'd certainly know if anyone was hiding in her room."

Prince had drunk enough liquor to be mulish. "He's hiding somewhere in this hotel. How do we know she isn't hiding him? They came in on the same train. I saw him carrying her bags. Go ahead, Appley, unlock the door."

"I'll open it," Alice Austin called, her anger carrying through the thickness of the door. "I'll open it." She crossed the room swiftly, barely giving the fat man time to drop down behind the head of the bed. Twisting the key, she pulled the door wide.

In the shaft of light from the hall, George Pitman had a full look at her, at the thin white bed gown with its laced edges, at her bare ankles and toes. He heard Tom Appley's quick-drawn breath and the marshal's jumbled apology, then Appley reached in and pulled the door closed saying, "I guess Prince has made a mistake."

"I guess he has," she called through the door, "and I'll certainly not forget to tell the Major."

George Pitman rose slowly from his place beside the head of the bed. He heard the searching party move on to the next room, then the next. Then he heard something else in the darkness. For a moment he thought the girl was crying, then he realized that she was laughing, almost hysterically.

"Their faces," she gasped in a stifled whisper. "I never saw anything so funny as their expression when I opened that door. A bold bunch of men to run from a woman in her nightgown. A bold bunch of men indeed."

14

At eleven o'clock Sam Allen
appeared at Nan Ireland's house, his face white, his mouth
tight with worry, his ink-stained printer's hands gripping
a heavy shotgun. He wasted few words in telling them how
he had sent for Jet, of talking to young Cosgrave in his
kitchen, then sending him to the dressmaker's house. He
had not known until a few minutes before that Jet had been
set upon in the alley by the Major's crew.

"No one knows where he is now," Allen said wearily,
"but he must be in town, and they're searching for him."

Judy went into the other room after her rifle. She came
back, moving toward the door, but Nan Ireland said quickly: "You can't do anything. Please stay here."

The redheaded girl looked at her. "I can still shoot,"
she said, "and if Cal Prince thinks he's going to have a
hanging he'd better think again." She moved to the door
without further words, and a moment later Allen limped
after her. Judy gave him one long look, then they left the
house in silence and moved down the street. The boy Steve
came out of the darkness with his terse report.

"They ain't caught him yet. They're searching the Colton House," then he vanished, leaving them to move on up
the street.

They paused a block from the hotel, watching the make-
shift posse leave the entrance and cross to the Palace
Saloon, the marshal with them, arguing with Prince. A
few minutes later the marshal came out alone and moved
toward them, an old man who had been in the country
since the first Indian days. He came up Fremont and found
Sam Allen and Judy watching him as he approached. His
mind was a card catalogue of the town, of its friendships

116

and its jealousies, and he remembered the printer as Jet Cosgrave's oldest friend. The girl and her rifle were also well known, and he realized suddenly that if Prince and his men cornered Cosgrave there would be at least two guns in town to stand against them.

He moved up into the shadow of the building before which they stood, saying in an undertone as he passed: "They haven't found him yet. I'll be at my office when they do." Then he moved on to his small office beyond the Banner House, and they saw his shadow through the front window as he took up a position to watch the street, a rifle across his old knees.

At daylight the Circle C moved out, apparently convinced that Jet had escaped them, and the girl turned back toward Nan Ireland's to freshen up before reporting to work.

At nine o'clock, as she moved along the hall of the Colton House, tidying the rooms, she came to the door of No. 8 and knocked lightly. Receiving no answer, she used the master key and stepped into the room. The curtains were drawn, and she did not realize that the room was occupied until she saw Alice Austin asleep in the chair, a blanket wrapped about her shoulders. Surprised, Judy glanced toward the bed and saw Jet's face. She guessed at once what had happened and stood for an instant motionless, then opened the door softly, peering up and down the hall. It was empty, so she closed the door quickly and moved lightly to the bed. Years of taking care of herself had made her self-reliant, and she had seen too many people injured to be affected by the sight of the dried blood. She bent over, finding his wrist and fingering his pulse; then she turned and found that Alice was awake, watching her, eyes wide with fear.

"Who are you? How'd you get in here?" The city girl threw aside her blanket and came quickly to her feet.

"The maid," said Judy. "He needs a doctor."

"No. There are men outside, waiting to kill him."

"They're gone," said Judy. "They rode out at daylight. How'd he get here?"

Alice Austin had not yet recovered from the shock of waking and finding her in the room. She gestured toward the window. "Over the roofs."

"And you kept him all night. Thank you." Judy had a directness that was disconcerting to those who did not know her. She swung toward the door.

"Wait. What are you going to do?"

"Get a doctor." The mountain girl was impatient. "He needs one bad."

"I—I was afraid to call one last night."

"Lucky you didn't." She was gone before Alice Austin could answer. For a moment the city girl stared at the closed door, then turned and moved over to the bed. She knew little of sick people, but Cosgrave seemed to be breathing normally. Then she dressed.

She had hardly finished when the door opened and Judy slid in, carrying a tray. She set it on the stand, saying as she did so: "I told Mrs. Appley you weren't feeling well and that I'd bring your breakfast up. I had her send for Doc Eaton and I sent a note to Sam Allen. He's Jet's friend."

Alice was watching her. "You—you know Jet?" She nodded toward the bed.

Judy pulled a gun from her apron pocket, balancing it with satisfaction. "Got this from the desk. Just in case . . ." Then she answered the other girl's question. "Know him? I'm going to marry him."

Alice Austin gasped. "You—you take things very quietly. I mean you don't get excited."

Judy looked surprised. "Excited? Well . . ." She thought it over for a minute in silence. "I guess you've just got to take things as they come; besides, he's a lot better lying here, even if he's hurt, than he would have been if Prince had found him."

There was a movement from the bed and she swung quickly around, her face lighting, suddenly transformed. "Jet."

"Judy." He was staring at her weakly.

"Hush," she said, her tone softer than it had been since

she had entered the room. "The doctor's on his way. Every-thing's all right." She bent and kissed his cheek.

His voice sounded weak and strained. "The Circle C?"

"They rode out."

He turned a little restlessly, his eyes searching the room, stopping when he saw Alice Austin.

"Now I remember. I crawled through your window."

"And she kept you," said Judy. "Prince searched the town, but I guess he didn't search here."

She was interrupted by a knock. Freeing her gun, she moved quickly to the door. It was the doctor and she let him in, locking the door after him. He was a small man, plump and bustling. He crossed the room and stood over the bed.

"So here's where you were, and the town searching for you. What are you trying to do, Jet, turn yourself into a punching bag?"

"It wasn't my idea," said Cosgrave, and tried to rise.

The doctor pushed him back. "Lie still a minute. I brought you into the world and I swear to the Lord you haven't been quiet a minute since. Let's have a look."

He had his look, both girls watching him in silence. When he finished he dressed the cut across the stomach, shaking his head as he did so.

"No broken ribs. You must have been made of rubber, judging by the bruises you got. Maybe the beating knocked some sense into you, but I doubt it."

"When can I get out of here?"

The doctor squinted at him. "Suppose I told you to spend a couple of days in bed?"

"I haven't the time."

"No." The doctor shook his head slowly. "You haven't the time. You're in too much of a hurry to get out and be shot. Well, my advice is for you to stay holed up here until after dark, then break for the hills. You're charged with murdering the Kid, you know."

"Six of them jumped me."

The doctor shrugged. "I have nothing to do with the

law or with your quarrels. But the Major won't let you rest, nor will Cal Prince."

"I can't stay here. It wouldn't be fair to Miss Austin."

"It wouldn't be fair if you left now. Someone is bound to see you; and if you slip out after dark, no one needs to know that you were here." He turned, picked up his bag, and headed for the door.

15

Hearing the sound of his ar-riving crew, the Major stepped briskly into the yard, his critical eyes noting that the horses had been driven hard and that the men were surly and tired. He frowned, sensing that they had failed before Cal Prince swung from the saddle and stalked toward him.

"Well?"

"He killed the Kid." The words burst from Prince. "We had him cornered in the alley, and the Kid wanted to rough him up before we turned him over to the marshal. He killed the Kid."

The Major was thoroughly angry. "Isn't there anything that you can do right? I should have gone myself. Rankin warns us that Jet will be in town, alone, and I send you with half a dozen men. He kills one of you and gets away. How?"

Prince turned sullen under the words. "We did exactly what you told us," he said. "We rode into town and kept out of sight, but we watched the livery stable. After dark that redheaded kid of Allen's came in leading a strange horse. We guessed then that your nephew was at the print-er's and we watched the house. When he came out, we cornered him. It was all too easy."

"And?" The Major was tense now.

"And the Kid fought him and Jet killed him. I'm telling you he's a wildcat, but if I ever get my hands on him again I'll break him apart. I promise that." The words were pushed out of Prince by his rising hate. "He killed Bert with Bert's own knife."

The Major's mouth had tightened and his eyes were bleak. "What then?"

121

"Then nothing," said Prince. "He got away. He crawled through a window into Saddler's store and went out the skylight and over the roof. He left a trail of blood."

"But you didn't get him?" The words were an indictment.

Prince bridled at the implication of failure. "We did our best." His tone was resentful. "We combed the block. I still can't figure where he got to. We even searched the Colton House, and did Tom Appley ask for trouble. He made me bring the marshal and Mather made me swear out a warrant. The whole town is laughing at Circle C this morning."

The Major's own temper was flaming, but he held it in check. Part of his anger was directed at Prince. He was a man who would not accept failure himself, nor tolerate it in others, and the idea of anyone laughing at the outfit made him writhe inwardly. None of this, however, showed in his cold voice.

"Never mind that. As soon as you get cleaned up, take the crew up to the Newmark. If Rankin has pulled out, take back the camp. There's more than one way of handling Jet. Alone he can't cause us much trouble. Sooner or later we'll lay hands on him."

Prince started to turn away, but the Major thought of something else. "You didn't disturb Miss Austin when you searched the hotel, did you?"

Prince stopped. He spoke, not looking at the ranch owner.

"We—" He broke off, hunting words.

The Major took a step toward him. "You what?"

"Well, she opened her door and . . ." Prince did not know exactly what to say. The liquid courage which had sustained him during the search was dying in his blood, leaving him jittery and not too confident. In his mind he damned all women for being unreasonable. "Well, we didn't mean any harm, but we knew he had to be hiding in one of the rooms and . . ."

"And what?" The Major's face had gone white. "I suppose you broke her door down. Was she in bed?"

"Well, not quite." Prince was thoroughly miserable. "But she wasn't quite dressed either."

The Major hit him. He'd been holding the heavy riding gloves in his hands, and he slammed them across Prince's face. "I should kill you."

Prince took the blow without moving. Only his small eyes seemed to glitter as he stared at the Major.

"You shouldn't have done that."

Cosgrave fought for control. "All right. Get cleaned up and then ride up to the line camp. If you find Jet, hang him; but whatever happens I expect you to take that camp." He swung away then, walking quickly toward the corral, apparently unconscious of Prince's brooding eyes.

He cut out his own horse, saddled it, and took the trail toward town. Behind him the watching crew turned slowly toward the cook shack. Prince was sullen as he ate. His anger at the Major burned deep, but his loyalty to the ranch was stronger than his resentment. When they had finished, he ordered them back into the saddle. With almost the full crew at his back, he took the trail toward the hills.

16

It was late morning before the Major reached Colton. He stabled his horse at Shorham's and moved up Linden toward the Colton House, pausing twice in his passage to raise his hat to the people he met. His face was serene, and from his cheerful expression no watcher could have guessed how his anger burned within him, or that his eyes searched each face for a hint of mockery.

To Linton Cosgrave life had always presented an interesting gamble. From late childhood he had spent it mostly in the saddle, with Jeb Stuart and then on this wide-flung range. He had learned early that a man is judged by his actions, his manner, and his appearance. He had no family feeling about his nephew. He had resented the boy from the first, since Jet would inherit the Circle C, and he had arranged to have the boy sent east to school, to get him away from the ranch. His sole thought then had been to take over the Circle C. But in the last year those plans had broadened. From the moment he had met Alice Austin he had wanted her, yet he had had to wait for the proper moment before pressing his suit. That moment had come with her father's failure and death. She had been utterly alone, and naturally she had turned to him. They would have been married in Chicago had not pressing business called him back to the Territorial capital. But he was still not certain of her, and now Prince's action of the night before filled him with unease. He turned into the Colton House, found the lobby empty, and climbed the stairs quickly, pausing to knock on the door of No. 8.

Inside he heard the rustle of silk, heard her voice say a little uncertainly, "Who is it?"

"Lin." She called him Lin. She was the only person in the world who did. To all others he was the Major, even to his few friends.

For a long instant there was silence behind the door, then she said breathlessly, "I'm—I'm not feeling well."

The Major's first thought was: She's angry. She's punishing me because Prince broke into her room. It was time to straighten that out now. His voice was firm, a little commanding.

"Come, Alice. Open the door."

Inside the room Alice Austin glanced quickly at the man on the bed. Jet was throwing back the covering blanket. He used the edge of the bed to pull himself to his feet, standing for a moment, testing his uncertain balance, then crossed the room and picked up the gun that Judy had left on the washstand. He broke it open, examined the loads, then retreated into the corner as the fat salesman had done, so that the opening door would conceal him. He nodded to the girl then, his lips forming the silent words: "Go with him. He'll stand there until you do."

She nodded her understanding, caught up a soft shawl, draped it around her shoulders, and moved to turn the key in the lock. Opening the door a little, she said: "I'm sorry, Lin. Shall we go down and talk?"

He stared at her, noting the dark circles under her fine eyes, her lack of color; and the thought occurred to him that she was ill. Prince had upset her. Aloud he said: "Of course not. You're in no shape to go anywhere. We'll talk here."

He saw her desperate hesitation and misunderstood. "After all, my dear, we'll be married tomorrow, and you needn't worry. In this town no one will think ill of my wife even if she does entertain men in her room." He smiled at his little joke, put out a hand, and gave the door a push.

She had been standing in the opening, holding the door lightly with one hand. His push tore it loose from her fingers and sent it back against the wall. The Major stepped in, and there was nothing for her to do but let him pass.

He turned to face her, and as he did so his eyes met those of his nephew across the girl's head.

Jet stood braced in the corner, the gun which Judy had stolen from Tom Appley held loosely in his left hand. He watched his uncle with mocking eyes, and the smile that hovered about his mouth was sardonic.

He said softly, "Shut the door, Alice."

She obeyed. She looked neither at the Major nor at Jet. It was as if she understood that this moment belonged to them, that she could have no part in it. Then she stepped back quickly and her questioning eyes turned to study Linton Cosgrave's face, as if to read an answer there, a reassurance which she needed in this moment.

"So that's it." They were the first words the Major used; but his tone told nothing and his face gave no indication of the raging anger that had suddenly seized him. A lesser man would have been shaken by its violence, but even now, in what he realized was one of the big crises of his life, Linton Cosgrave held himself under restraint.

"So Prince was right. You *were* hiding behind a woman's skirts."

Jet Cosgrave crowded down his impulse to laugh. He understood fully how his uncle felt. He knew that Linton looked on Alice's act as one of treachery. You simply did not desert your own outfit to give comfort to the enemy. The only explanation the Major could understand was that the girl had changed sides, that perhaps she loved his nephew.

Jet said slowly, "I'd hide behind anything, Major, to get away from your hired killers."

"I didn't send them to kill you. I ordered them to turn you over to the marshal." The Major was surprised by his own words. He had no intention of justifying his position to anyone, but the girl made a difference. He had not expected her to relish the fighting, but he had not dreamed that she might be on the other side.

Jet gave him a thin smile. "When you're jumped in the dark, you do your best to protect yourself. No matter what your orders, I'd be buzzard bait now if it hadn't been for Miss Austin."

The girl spoke then without moving. "Those men were drunk. They were bent on murder."

The Major answered without taking his eyes from his nephew's face. "I didn't start this fight. You've got to understand that this isn't the East. We have no law, no government here to protect us and what we own. We have to protect ourselves in any way we can."

"By murder?"

He shifted under the fire of her bitterness, but he still spoke in a low tone and unhurriedly. "I didn't start this trouble," he repeated. "Ask the young man you've protected why he came to Colton. Ask him about the crew he brought in. Ask him about seizing my line camp, killing the man who held it. Ask him if he expected me to welcome him with open arms."

"I'm not asking him," she said steadily. "I didn't come a thousand miles to marry him. I came here to marry you, and I think I have a right to question the kind of man my future husband is."

He glanced at her momentarily, and his face softened. She was so very beautiful, so very desirable, so proud and demanding and unafraid.

Jet saw the change and was shocked. He had thought that the Major had wanted her as he'd want to own a beautiful horse or a valuable ranch. Now he saw that it was more than that, much more. He perceived that she had a power over the Major that no one else had ever had, a power to reach him, to move him, yes, to break him. He knew, too, that the Major hated him, not as he had hated him before, but as he would hate any man he found talking to her, any man who could make her smile or cause her eyes to light.

The Major's control was cracking a little as he tried to answer her. "I'm no different than I ever was. I'm the same as I was that day in Chicago, the day you promised to marry me."

"Yes," she said slowly, and she sounded sad. "That's

what I'm afraid of. I had to come here to realize that. I'm afraid it's a mistake. Perhaps's it's a good thing for me that this has happened, that I found out in time."

The Major cracked wide open, and he turned the full power of his rage against the silent man in the corner.

"So you've stolen her too. You weren't content with taking the line camp, with trying to ruin the Circle C. You've stolen her. But you won't live to enjoy the theft; that I solemnly swear to you."

Jet stared at him. For five years he had planned to wreck this man, and as the years passed his hatred of his uncle had grown until it was an all-consuming passion; but never in his wildest moments had he ever dreamed of hurting the Major as he was being hurt now. The Major loved the Circle C, and its loss would be gall and wormwood to him, but to lose the girl . . . Jet looked at her and wondered at her power, and felt it touch him also. She was beautiful and warm and lovely. A man could not find a woman like her in many a long day's ride. Why not take her from the Major, marry her himself, flaunt her in the older man's face before he killed him? Then he rebelled against the idea. No man of any decency would do such a thing. It would be a poor way to repay her kindness and her courage. It was something the country might contemptuously expect of the Major, of a Cosgrave. Well, he thought, I am a Cosgrave, and it will take a Cosgrave to beat the Major, someone as ruthless as he is. Was it worse to marry this girl than to bring in Rankin and his men, to turn them loose in the hills, killing and plundering? He couldn't stop now. And besides, what was wrong with marrying her? Certainly he would be as good a husband as the Major would, and she had been willing to desert all she knew to come here to marry the Major. Then the thought of Judy rushed into his mind, but he swept it out. Judy wasn't for him. She was sweet and good, and a man could want her desperately, but she did not fit the pattern of his plans. Everything must stand aside for his vengeance. He had made his decision.

He said, a little harshly: "I've been threatened before. If

Miss Austin would have me, I'd be proud. No, don't try it, Major." The big gun in his hand steadied on the third button of the Major's vest, and the girl threw him a startled look.

The Major's face was very white, but he did not move. "Go ahead. Kill me."

"Not here," said Jet, and his voice turned mocking. "It isn't affection for you that stops me, but the fact that your body might cause Alice embarrassment. I'm going to ride out."

The Major breathed deeply, still trying to control himself. "And you think I'll stand aside now and let you go?"

"You will," Jet said, "or I'll have to change my mind and kill you here. Use your left hand and drop that gun belt."

Their eyes locked and Jet read refusal forming in his uncle's eyes. He moved with startling speed. He took two quick steps, brought the heavy barrel of the gun down across Lin Cosgrave's head, and watched the older man slip quietly to the floor.

The girl cried out sharply, and Jet said, "I'm sorry, but it was that or kill him." On a sudden impulse, and without words he bent forward and kissed her. She was too startled to pull away. His last picture was of her eyes, enormous, surprised, and filled with utter disbelief, but as he reached the hall and moved quickly to the stairs he put the girl out of his mind. The one thing of importance now was to get out of town.

The lobby was deserted, and he crossed it to the street without seeing anyone. He went to the livery, where he found his horse already saddled. He had covered several miles before he remembered that he had not had the chance to say goodbye to Judy. He owed her so much. It was she who had brought the doctor and the gun, she who had seen to it that his horse was saddled, waiting for him to ride out.

17

Dude Rankin wasted no time
after seeing Jet ride away with the redheaded boy. He sent
the crew headlong into the brush, and before the hour was
out they were working small gathers of steers down from
the rocky draws into the main valley. By dark they had almost fifteen hundred head, mostly long threes, and Rankin
made no effort to hide his satisfaction. "We'll push them a
couple of miles and bed down. In the morning we'll start
for the pass."

"What if young Cosgrave shows up?" It was Curly, the
cook.

Rankin started to say that Jet Cosgrave was not likely to
show up, then checked himself. "Never mind him; we have
a better claim to this herd than he does. We've got the bill
of sale from Prince."

A second man said slowly, "That trail's mighty rough."

Rankin turned on him. "You're damn' right it's rough.
We'll lose some critters on the way over, but we'll get most
of them across, more than enough to give each of us a
stake. We'll sell them on the reservation to the Indian
agent. Curly, get a chuck outfit together."

Curly stood resolute. Rankin took a step toward him,
saying: "You heard me. I want no trouble from you."

There was a rifle leaning against the cookshack wall.
Curly caught it up, saying steadily, "There won't be no
trouble unless you start it."

Color came up in Rankin's leathery cheeks. "Look, old
man, I've got something else to think of besides killing you.
Stay if you want to. Wait for young Cosgrave." His smile
turned wicked. "Anyone else?"

Shay said, "Me, maybe."

Rankin frowned. "What's the matter? Afraid of work?"

The man said slowly: "I made a deal with young Cosgrave. He hasn't done anything to break it."

Rankin stared at him for a moment, then swung to his horse. "Stay here, then. I hope you both get gut-shot."

The two men stood silently watching the herd being pushed up the valley to the bed ground, then they looked at each other. It was Curly who said, "Me, I think we'd be safer sleeping in the brush."

Shay nodded and together they went after their horses, riding up into the timber, where they made a fireless camp. In the morning chill they huddled uncomfortably on the rocks, watching the men below them put the herd into motion.

"Maybe we made a mistake," Shay grumbled, made sour by the cold and the lack of food. "Young Cosgrave didn't show up last night. Maybe he's been bushwhacked."

"Maybe," said Curly, watching Rankin's wranglers drive the horses from the corral below and push them after the vanished herd. "But me, I'd rather take my chances than ride along with Dude Rankin. You never can tell what Dude will think to do, and he hates being crossed. Young Cosgrave backed him down, so he sells out to this Major. Next time it might be me, or you, or both of us he'd sell out. Damn a man who don't stay hitched." He broke off, having talked much longer than was his wont, and fumbled in his pockets. Finding a frayed tobacco plug, he worried off a corner with his old teeth, and passed the plug to Shay. They chewed in displeased silence, having had neither supper nor breakfast. Finally Shay stood up, easing the cramp from his stiff muscles.

"To hell with it," he said. "They're gone. I'm going down and eat."

He turned and walked to their picketed horses, and after a minute Curly rose and followed. As they swung up, the cook said: "You can ride after the crew. They haven't made more than a couple of miles, and they're traveling slow. Rankin will probably forget how you acted. He's smart enough to know they can use an extra hand. He'll need all the help he can get before he shoves those cow critters through that pass."

Shay threw him a sullen look. "No," he said slowly. "Win or lose, I guess I'll play the hand out without Dude Rankin. I've had enough of him."

The cook nodded his solemn agreement. "I kind of like this country," he said. "It's softer than those northern places, and it don't get so cold in the winter.

"The long trail is O.K. when you're young, and I've raised my share of hell and had some fun; but when a man gets to a certain point he likes to pull off his boots now and then and shove his sock feet under a hot stove."

"Yeah," said Shay. Pushing out of the brush, he passed the remnants of the old stockade, crossed the yard, and turned his mount free in the deserted corral. "Rankin might have left us a couple of spare mounts."

"Not Dude," said Curly, and freed his own horse of the saddle.

Shay leaned against the fence. "Have you figured what to do if Cosgrave does come back? The crew is gone, and three men can't fight the Circle C."

"You think too much," said Curly. "I'm just a cook. I don't need to think."

"Maybe you'd better start," Shay warned. "Suppose Cosgrave doesn't ever come back. Suppose he has been killed like I said. Where in hell is he, anyway?"

"You know," said Curly, "maybe I'm wrong. But since you ask me, I'll tell you what I think. I think he's got a girl. He acted last night as if he had a girl on his mind."

Shay spat through his broken teeth into the dust at his feet and began to curse. When he'd exhausted his vocabulary twice, he summed up: "A fine thing. No crew, the boy with women on his mind, and us here like a couple of sitting ducks just waiting for those Circle C coyotes to drop in here and put a rope around our necks."

"If you feel that way," Curly told him, "you'd better ride. Me, I'm going to eat." He turned and walked across the yard to disappear into the cookshack without waiting for an answer.

Shay hesitated, looked after him, then looked back at his horse in the corral. He hitched his belt twice and straightened his broken hat.

"To hell with it," he muttered, and followed the cook.

The morning dragged. They spent the time cleaning up the mess the departing crew had made of the main house, then checked over the supplies that were left and broke out a can of peaches, which they shared. At noon they ate under the tree. By this time Curly's nerves were beginning to show.

"Wonder what happened to the boss? A man can spend a night with a girl, but I thought he'd be back before now."

Shay grunted. The pressure of waiting was telling on him too. "If he doesn't come by dark, I'm pulling out."

Curly looked skeptical. "Think Rankin will let you join up after all this time?"

"To hell with Rankin. I'm just riding out."

"If Cosgrave doesn't show by evening," the cook decided, "I'll go with you."

His announcement seemed to reassure Shay. He cleaned his plate, then went into the house and rolled into his bunk. Curly looked in on him twice and finally went to the cookshack. He was there when the Circle C rode up, and he put his head out in time to see Cal Prince studying the corral.

"They've pulled out, all right. Look at the tracks." Prince spoke to Sawyer, who was riding at his side.

"Someone's here." Sawyer nodded to the two ponies in the corral.

"Maybe young Cosgrave." Prince's weariness dropped away before his eagerness and he swung his horse around, calling a sharp order, then turned to stare at the buildings in time to see Curly reaching from the cookshack door for his rifle, which leaned against the outer wall. Before he stopped to consider, Prince swung his own gun up and threw a shot at the cook. He missed as Curly dived back inside; but the crew, taking their cue from the foreman, were pouring bullets into the old logs as fast as they could pump their rifle levers.

Shay came out of a sound sleep at the first shot, hit the floor without bothering to pull on his boots, grabbed up his rifle, and jumped toward the window. His first bullet knocked down a man on Prince's right, and the foreman shouted above the racket of the guns, "Spread out, hit the timber."

Ten men veered away to the east while five followed Prince in his headlong dash for cover. Curly got one of the racing horses, but the rider rolled over and came up running, hitting the edge of the brush where the valley's rising side climbed toward the western hogback. The cook's reaching bullets pursued him into the timber but failed to find their mark.

There was a lull. The men in the house could see nothing to shoot at. Prince was in no hurry. He reasoned that Cosgrave was in the house with one man in the cookshack. Rankin and the crew had apparently pulled out. All he had to do was wait. Time was on their side. Ordering the men beside him to maintain enough fire to hold those in the building forted up, he turned his horse south, riding beyond rifle range until he crossed the valley and came into the timber on the eastern side. Here he found his ten men dismounted, their horses picketed in a small clearing, while the riders fanned out along the edge of the trees facing the house. Between them and the line of the old stockade fence was the winding stream, cutting down through the meadow between four-foot banks. The banks offered shelter, and there was enough of the stockade still standing to give some cover to any who could reach it.

Prince's plan was quickly made. There had been no sign of Cosgrave outside the house, but he still felt certain that he had the Major's nephew pinned down at last. He ordered Sawyer, whom he put in charge, to wait until he gave the signal, then to send out men to the stream bank. That accomplished, he returned the way he had come.

Both Curly and Shay could see him as he recrossed the lower valley, and Curly sent a wishful bullet winging toward the foreman, although he knew that the range was too long for effective shooting. But he had the pleasure of seeing Cal Prince bend low and heel his horse to a plunging gallop, and he yelled from sheer excitement.

Shay yelled back. They could not see each other, but less than thirty feet separated their positions. "What did I tell you about staying, Curly?"

The cook swore at him.

"Suppose they'd let us ride out if we surrender?"

"They'd hang us."

"I guess so." Shay saw a man running for the river and snapped a shot. The man went down in the deep grass, but Shay was certain that he'd missed, knowing that the shot had been too high.

Curly had seen the movement and cut loose. "They're trying to make the river. If they get across and behind the old stockade, we're dead ducks for certain."

"We're dead anyhow," Shay called back. He was sweating in the hot air of the house. "As soon as it gets dark enough, they'll sneak in; that is, if we last until dark."

"We can sneak out then." Curly was hopeful. "The moon comes up late."

"That's right." There was new hope in Shay's voice. "If we can get into the brush . . ." He sent a shot at the trees, then there was a lull.

A shot sounded in the timber to the west, then a sudden scrambled chorus of yells. Both defenders tightened the grip on their guns, awaiting an expected charge. None came. Instead there was another shot, farther back in the timber, then silence, and afterward a full fusillade.

18

The first miles out of town were torture to Jet, but he had slept thoroughly, from sheer exhaustion; and as the exercise loosened his muscles and the heat of the sun drew out some of the aching soreness, he began to enjoy the ride. He cut across country, rising and falling with the uneven contour of the land and angling eastward to avoid crossing the Circle C. This brought him at noon to the mouth of the Main Beldos canyon and he paused to water his horse, then turned into the trail which led northeastward into Lone Star.

Only a ridge separated the mining-town trail from the Newmark Valley and he could cross it at any point he chose. The trail was rutted deep from the heavy wheels of the big freight wagons that hauled supplies to the mining camp from the distant railroad, and it made easier traveling than working his way through the brush. It was also the main trail northeast, passing the mining town and climbing steeply in sharp corkscrews until it reached the rocky crest of the Munyards, then winding westward across the corner of the reservation to pick up the canyon of the Moccasin.

It was over this rough trail that Rankin and his crew had come into the country; and if they lost their battle with the Major, it was over this trail that they would all have to retreat. But Cosgrave had no intention of losing the battle. Things were working out much better and faster than he had hoped. He would not only seize the ranch; he would break the Major as no man had ever been broken, using the girl as a tool. Then the possibility that she might not marry him filled him with sudden doubts.

Maybe she won't, he thought, but I can try; and the effect on the Major will be the same. I'm a louse. I'm mixing things up for two women; but I didn't intend it that way, and I can't stop now. I have to play the cards as they are dealt to me.

But the nagging feeling of deep guilt wouldn't down, and it made him angry with himself.

I've got a conscience, he thought. Sam Allen was right, damn him. I've got a conscience, the first Cosgrave to have one, I guess; but to the devil with it. You can't win a war if you worry about the people who might get hurt. I won't worry about Alice and I certainly won't worry about Judy. I've got my hands full worrying about this fight.

His reverie broke as he heard noise ahead. Turning off quickly, he pulled into the shelter of some trees to sit quietly and watch while five lumbering freight outfits crept past; then he pulled back into the trail, letting his horse choose its own gait.

At one o'clock he angled off to the left, following a small side draw that wound upward through the thickening timber toward the rocky shoulder separating Newmark Valley from the main canyon. He climbed slowly, seeking the easiest path, but was twice forced by rock slides to turn back. This was a rugged section, piled with splintered boulders which had rested there so long that giant pines grew over them, putting down roots which almost hid the stones and searching through the cracks for earth enough to give them support and sustenance. It had always puzzled Cosgrave that the ridge should be so rough on the east slope while to the west it descended much more gently into Newmark Valley.

He reached the summit finally and started downward, the growth so heavy that it was difficult for his horse to find passage. And then the first shots came up out of the valley below, the flat smacking reports of rifle fire. He stopped to localize the action; but the sound of the guns spread as if the whole upper valley were filled with fighting men, and he cursed under his breath.

He had not expected a battle, having left the Major in town; and yet this was no small skirmish, as Prince's first attack had been. He tried to count the shots and failed, for they blended into one another. Here and there, above the crescendo of action, it seemed that he could hear muffled shouts, but they were a long way off. He goaded his horse quickly but left the rifle in its boot, knowing that it would be fifteen or twenty minutes at best before he could reach the valley floor.

As they descended, the small scrubby trees which had seemed laced together gave way. The trees became larger, their trunks perhaps a foot through, while their green tops towered above him, cutting off the sun. His horse's feet made no sound on the thick mantle of long needles that cloaked the ground, and a little lower he broke out into small grassed patches where the sunlight managed to filter downward to the earth.

The firing ahead had not ceased but had dropped to an occasional shot, as if one side had forted up while the other sniped from a safe distance. He halted again, sitting very still in the saddle, bending forward to catch each sound the wind might bring.

A gun spoke to his right, and he judged it to be not more than half a mile away. He loosened the rifle from the scabbard and rode on, carefully now, not crossing an open glade until his eyes had examined the timber on all sides. He had no desire to fall into an ambush. Working gradually forward, he struck the floor of the valley a good half mile below the ranch buildings and dismounted, tethering his horse and then stepping to the timber edge to have his look. For a few moments there was little to see. Then a rifle flashed from the bush on the west to be answered by a shot from the cookshack and a second from the log house.

Stillness settled on the echoes. A fly buzzed around Cosgrave's head with insistent vigor, and he swung his lame arm to ward it off. Whoever the attackers were, they were well screened, for he could see no one. What bothered him was the corral. It was all but empty. He thought that the crew must be riding somewhere; but if they were, why hadn't the shots brought them in? Then his worried eye caught movement across the valley on the west. A man had left the line of trees. He ran a few feet toward the house, bent over so sharply that he hardly showed above the tall grass; but he had been seen from the house. A rifle spat angrily and he dropped, although Cosgrave did not think he had been hit. In a moment he knew that his guess was right, for the man was up again, crawling toward the shelter of the old stockade. Then a second man appeared, this time from the east, and edged his careful way forward. He reached the creek without drawing fire and dropped from sight below the high cutbank.

Cosgrave wondered if he ought to leave his horse and work northward along the timber fringe. As he debated he saw another man rush for shelter of the creek bed. And now half a dozen guns broke into steady action west of the house. He frowned. It was obvious that this barrage was intended to distract the defenders so that the men by the creek could come up behind the old stockade. If this succeeded, the house and cookshack would be flanked on two sides.

He swung back to his horse, and as he mounted he cursed Rankin in a steady undertone. Where was the trail boss? Where were the rest of the crew? From the firing he judged that there was one man trapped in the house and one in the cook shack. He looped back into the wood, thinking that the besiegers would be concentrated along its edge and that his chances of approach were bettered by staying deep within the trees.

He advanced rapidly but cautiously, urged on by the now constant splatter of guns. Suddenly he stopped, listening, for ahead he had heard the restless stir of horses. He swung down. Leaving the rifle beside his mount, he drew Tom Appley's short gun and pressed ahead stealthily. After traveling about fifty yards, he paused again as he came upon a group of horses in a little clearing. For a moment he could see no one guarding them, then realized that there was a man on the far side, his back to the restless animals, his full attention on the valley below.

Cosgrave considered. The easiest thing was to shoot the jingler down. He offered a perfect target, the back of his sweat-stained gray shirt showing clear and distinct between the branches of the trees. But caution stopped him. Instead he crept around the clearing, his gun ready, the stomping of the horses covering the sound of his movements. He was within half a dozen feet of the wrangler when the man sensed his presence and began to turn.

Cosgrave covered the distance in two bounds, and as the man came around Jet smashed the heavy revolver down across the rider's weather-stained hat. The man's gun had been half drawn. He dropped it and without a sound followed it to the ground, landing squarely on his face, and lay still.

Jet peered through the trees, searching for a second guard, saw none, and turned to the horses. He had no knife and had to go back to the unconscious man for one. He picked up the wrangler's gun, pitched it into the brush, then slashed the pickets and beat the animals away with his flapping hat. The horses broke free with a whinnying charge, scattering in all directions, pulling out through the brush. Cosgrave turned toward his own mount as a voice behind him shouted suddenly, "Joe! Joe!" and a man thrashed toward him. "Joe, what happened?"

He saw Cosgrave then, and stopped, bringing up his rifle, firing as he raised it, the bullet striking a tree on Cosgrave's left. As Jet shot him, he saw the man's arms go wide, saw him stumble, let the rifle go, and pitch headlong. His horse bucked away from the shot and he had to swing up while it was still dancing. Below him rose a medley of yells, and he drove away, angling toward higher ground. He had traveled a thousand yards when the flat spat of a rifle came from the brush at his right and his horse lunged and then buckled under him.

Cosgrave had only time to kick out of the stirrups and fling free of the horse. Then he was rolling over and over along the spongy bed of needles, coming to an abrupt stop against a tree. He wriggled around it, trying to put the solid trunk between him and the unseen marksman. His rifle lay beside the dead horse a dozen feet away. It might as well have been a hundred feet away for all the good it did him.

But he still had Tom Appley's gun; and he balanced it in his palm, trying to shake off the jar of his fall. Finally a voice reached him from behind a prone pine.

"Come out, Cosgrave, I've got you like a cornered rat."

"Who is it?" Jet could not identify the voice.

"Olf Polsen." The unseen man chuckled harshly. "I just wanted you to know before you die, that we'll have no Cosgrave hanging around our sister." He laughed, shrill and taunting. "Come out; that is, if you have the nerve."

19

Hugged down behind his sheltering tree, Cosgrave felt a shock run through his big body at the sound of the Polsen name. He had assumed that the shot that had killed his horse had come from a Circle C gun. It was serious enough to be cornered by his uncle's men, but to have the Polsens also in the thick timber, quiet as Indians and as vicious, doubled the odds against him. He lay a moment, panting, every sense alert. He did not know whether Olf was alone or whether the other brothers were somewhere on his flank, and the uncertainty kept him speechless.

The silence annoyed the unseen mountain man and he raised his voice until it was a sharp rasp. "Cosgrave. You hear me, Cosgrave. Stop playing possum. I want to talk before I finish you."

Jet still held his tongue, and after a moment Polsen called again. "Damn you for a yellow-bellied coward. You weren't hit; I know that. I knocked down your horse on purpose. Sing out. Why are you afraid to talk?"

Cosgrave said evenly: "Keep shouting, you fool, and you'll have the whole Circle C down on your neck. The woods are crawling with them."

There was a jeer in Polsen's tone. "Let them come. Cal Prince never saw the day he could dig me out, and he knows it."

"He will today," said Cosgrave, "if you keep yelling. I put them afoot, and they'll be singing around here like a bunch of bees. I wish I knew where my crew is."

"They're gone," Polsen called with relish. "I guess they sold you out. We watched them this morning, rounding up

142

the critters in the valley. They're headed out toward the pass."

Cosgrave found no surprise in the knowledge, but a slow, steady anger climbed in him. He had known that Dude Rankin was not one to trust, but the fact that the man had seized upon his absence to comb the valley and drive out the herd filled him with growing rage. The beef belonged to the Circle C. It was one thing for him to blot the brand, since in his heart he felt that the ranch was rightfully his, but quite another for a bunch of northern saddle tramps to ride off with Circle C cows. It was a direct blow at the ranch, and he found himself undergoing a curious reaction. No one could strike at the ranch—no one but a Cosgrave, that is. If outsiders tried it, they did so at their own risk. It was a lesson he meant to teach Dude Rankin. He did not pause to consider the position that the desertion of the crew had placed him in. His only thought was to reach Rankin, to bring back the herd.

Then, since the crew had gone, he wondered who was in the cookshack and the house. Could it be the two missing Polsen boys? But even as the thought occurred, he put it away. The Polsens would never have allowed themselves to be trapped inside a house. Who then? But that was of little importance. What mattered was that Rankin and his men were even now pushing Circle C beef toward the mountains. He was ridden by a violent impatience, which did not show in his voice.

"We've got a standoff," he called softly. "You've got a rifle against my short gun, but you can't get at me; and with the Circle C around, neither of us can wait long."

"Long enough." Polsen was not disturbed. "My brothers are at the upper end of the valley. They'll be back, and I'd hate to kill you before they get here to share the fun."

Jet did not answer, for he had seen brief movement behind the pine where Polsen lay. For an instant he thought it was one of the brothers returning, then he caught the glint of sunlight on a raised gun barrel. He brought up his own weapon, almost stepping into view. As he fired, the other gun cracked, the shots so closely spaced that they blended into one report. Polsen leaped upright, turning as he rose, his rifle spitting like an angry snake, and a Circle C rider tumbled out of the brush to fall almost at Polsen's feet.

Below them there was the sound of running men, their curses, and a loud cry of, "Hank! Oh, Hank!"

Cosgrave had moved as Polsen rose. He came around his tree, jumped forward, and shoved his gun against the mountain man's ribs. Polsen stood still, looking down at the puncher who lay on his face, unmoving. He seemed unaware of Cosgrave's gun against his side or of the blood welling out of the hole at the back of his shoulder. He took a long, deep breath.

Cosgrave said harshly, "We'd better get out of here, fast." He pulled his gun away and dropped it into his holster, then swung back with a quick step to catch up the rifle from beside his fallen horse. When he turned, Polsen was staring at him with unbelieving eyes.

"You had me," he said slowly, as if he could not understand a man who, holding him under a gun, turned away.

"*He* had you," said Jet. "It wouldn't have been your shoulder if I hadn't shot him. Can you walk?"

"It's my shoulder," said Polsen. "I don't walk on my shoulder."

"Then let's get going. If you still want to fight me when this is finished, I'll oblige." He turned without further words, ducked under the sweeping branches of the nearest tree, and strode up the grade, not even glancing around to see if Polsen followed.

They had traveled five minutes in silence, their feet making no sound on the needle cushion, when Olf's voice reached him, shaking a little: "I'm leaking from this shoulder. They can trail us unless it's plugged."

Cosgrave turned. He stood listening a full minute for sound of pursuit, then came back to the man's side. Polsen's face looked gray under his heavy tan, his breathing was labored, and the whole upper arm of his shirt was soaked with blood. Sweat stood out on his forehead and beaded his upper lip. One look and Cosgrave knew that the man was beat out, that he could not travel much farther.

Wordlessly he pulled out the knife he had taken from the wrangler and sliced away the shirt, using the lower part of it as a bandage, binding it in place with his own neckerchief. The bullet had entered the shoulder below the collarbone, making a neat, purple-edged hole, but its soft nose had spread, tearing away half of the shoulder blade. Cosgrave was a little sickened. He wondered how the man stayed on his feet.

He said: "You can't go far with that. Squat down somewhere and I'll try to lead them away."

He expected no thanks and he got none, but Polsen said suddenly, "They're coming now."

Cosgrave caught up the rifle Polsen had laid aside as a stick snapped somewhere below. Between the green branches he saw a quick flash of color from a man's shirt. He drove a bullet at it and heard the man's high yell.

"Go on," he shouted to Polsen. "Get to the top. Go on." He heard no sound, but when he looked the mountain man had vanished.

Below him all was quiet, but he sent a second bullet after the first and drew a shot in return. Satisfied that they had spotted him, he ducked about and ran, heedless of the sound he made as he crashed through the brush. The ground became steeper as he mounted higher on the ridge, and the growth was heavier. Behind him he heard the thrashing pursuit and knew that he had pulled them away from Polsen's trail.

He turned along the slope and went downhill, silent now, moving more carefully, seeking every inch of cover he could find as he worked northward, finally halting, thoroughly winded, at the edge of the trees, well above the ranch buildings. Before him lay the shining stream, and behind the farther cutbank he saw two men crouching. He raised his rifle and his bullet splattered the wet earth between them. They dropped into the water, yelling wildly, their shouts bringing a shot from the log house.

Cosgrave stepped back into the trees and worked north again toward the valley's head. He had traveled perhaps a sixteenth of a mile when shots broke out below him, and he returned to the edge of the trees for another look. Someone else was in the brush south of him, firing at the men in the stream; he saw them crowd down in the water until only their heads showed, trying desperately for cover. He wondered who this attacker was, then, hearing shots higher up the ridge, he guessed that the Polsen boys must have worked past him in the timber and joined the fight against the Circle C.

Prince heard the new firing and was puzzled by it. Swearing deeply, he mounted his four men. The fifth lay flat in the deep grass beside the stockade, pinned down by the guns from the house. The fight was going against them again, and Prince was raging. Not understanding what had happened, he raced his group south, intending to cross the valley and come to the aid of the crew on the east. But they never made it, for Cosgrave saw their maneuver and ran into the open, angling downward toward the house. As he ran he pumped a fresh shell into his gun and fired at the Circle C man in the grass beside the stockade.

The hidden man twisted, not liking the attack from this angle or the fact that his friends were apparently riding away. He came upright and raced for the trees, but he failed to reach them. Curly saw him rise and knocked him down before he had traveled half the distance, then turned and ran to the cookshack's rear window to learn who was north of the house.

He saw Cosgrave and flung out his high shrill yell of welcome. "The boss, Shay. The boss. I told you he'd come. I told you."

A sudden burst of fire barked from the east. They swung around and discovered that the shooting from the trees was not directed at them but at Prince and his men.

The Circle C riders jerked to a halt, and in that moment the two men who had been pinned in the stream leaped up and raced down the meadow, trying to join their mounted fellows. A single bullet from the brush knocked one over, but the second sprinted away and reached the horsemen. Catching a free stirrup, he swung up behind one of the riders. Prince sat hesitating, having no way of knowing how many of his men were still alive in the brush, or who was opposing them.

Curly raised his rifle, throwing a smattering of shots at the mounted men, and they pulled away, reluctant to leave, yet fearing his searching bullets. They spread, riding slowly toward the valley's lower end, looking back as if they expected their crew to boil out of the western timber to join them; but none came.

Cosgrave had rushed into the yard, meeting Curly and being joined a moment later by Shay. "Watch it," he called. "The Polsens are in that timber, and some of the Circle C. They're afoot, but they still have guns."

"Hell with them," said Shay, wiping his face.

Curly was trying to tell Cosgrave about Rankin and the herd that the trail boss was driving out.

Cosgrave nodded curtly. "I know." He was watching Prince and the five men with him. They were out of rifle range now, but they were still in the valley. He leaned against the house, trying to catch his breath, then said to Shay: "Neither of those horses in the corral seems to be hit. Get them up. The best thing we can do is ride out. There's still too many of them for us."

They looked at him, not understanding, since the fight seemed won. He told them: "Those jaspers shooting in the brush are Polsens. They're fighting the Circle C but they'd rather be fighting us." They still did not understand, but he wasted no breath trying to explain. "Get the horses. Don't argue."

Shay moved reluctantly toward the corral, and Cosgrave turned, watching the timber's edge to give the man what cover he could. As he turned he saw three horsemen break into the open, herding two men before them, and recognized the riders as the Polsens. He studied their approach, holding his rifle ready. Shay had halted beside the corral gate, leaning loosely against the pole fence, his rifle gripped in both hands. Curly stood on Cosgrave's right, his full attention centered on the advancing men, his lips beginning to curve in a slowly growing grin.

"Prisoners," he said. Then, recognizing one of the limping figures: "There's that jasper you wouldn't let us hang.
Maybe you'll change your mind now."

Cosgrave did not speak. He too had seen the limping
Sawyer. He glanced down the valley and saw that Prince's
crew had stopped and were watching the proceedings. Suddenly he wanted to laugh at them. Counting the Polsens,
there were six men and two prisoners. Prince had five men
besides himself, and two of them rode double on a horse.
The odds were evened, or better than evened. The Circle
C foreman must have judged this and made his galling
decision, for he raised his arm and swung away, his crew
following him in burning defeat.

With that pressure gone, Jet gave his full thought to the
approaching Polsens, wondering what their attitude would
be. The Circle C was bested and knew it; but Cosgrave
realized that he owed the valley to Polsen guns, and he
found no pleasure in the thought. He walked across the
yard, still carrying his rifle but letting it sag now, as if expecting that they came as friends. Stopping at the line of
the old stockade, he waited until the prisoners reached him.
They sank down in the dust as if they could go no farther
and no longer cared what happened. They were a sorry-
looking sight: both were wounded and the wrangler had
taken a gun whipping around the head. Cosgrave gave them
a momentary glance, then turned his attention to the riders.
Olf's whole side was soaked in blood, and he sat his horse
only because the brother on his right steadied him in the
saddle.

Cosgrave said, "Better get him to the house," and they
rode past without a word, stepping down, lifting Olf, and
carrying him into the room. Curly had come up, and Cosgrave turned the prisoners over to him, telling the cook to
get them indoors, then walked up to the house as the Polsens emerged. The first one out stopped, staring at him
without expression.

"We don't like you, Jet, but Olf told us how you pulled
those dogs off his trail."

Cosgrave ignored the remark and said, "There were four or five other men in the timber."

"Dead," said the taller Polsen. "We jumped them while they were hunting you. Olf got back to his horse. He wouldn't have made it if you hadn't pulled them away."

"He needs a doctor," Cosgrave said.

"A doctor isn't going to help." The tall one seemed unmoved. He looked at the sullen prisoners as Curly herded them forward. "What'll we do with them?"

Cosgrave hesitated. He walked to where Sawyer sat, propping himself upright in the lower bunk.

"How many were there?"

"Seventeen, with Prince." The man was bitter. "They told us your crew had pulled out."

Cosgrave looked at him sharply, then said slowly, "And only six rode away."

Sawyer did not answer, and Cosgrave said in a different tone, "How bad are you?"

The man's eyes had dulled. "Bad enough."

Cosgrave walked out to where Curly stood beyond the door. "Get a horse and ride to Colton. Find Doc Eaton and bring him back. Also, go to Nan Ireland's and tell Judy Polsen that one of her brothers is hurt and that she'd better come out with the doctor."

He felt the eyes of the silent Polsens watching him but he ignored them. "And be careful riding out. Circle C may have left some riders at the valley mouth."

"Those guys." The cook spat his contempt. "They can't fight for shucks." He turned and walked to the corral. Cosgrave went with him to meet Shay.

"You stay and watch the prisoners," he told the bow-legged man. "And Curly, bring out a couple of extra horses; tell Shorham that they're for me." Then he looked at Shay. "Get some grub together while I saddle up."

The little man looked at him. "Where you going, boss?"

"Why, after the herd. You don't think I'm going to let Dude Rankin ride out with my cows?"

Shay shook his head. "You didn't give Curly time to tell you. Dude's got a bill of sale for those critters. Cal

Prince slipped in night before last and made a deal. Your uncle bought off your crew with those cows."

Jet Cosgrave stared at him. His mind, dulled by fatigue, took seconds to understand the man's words; then he said slowly: "So that was it. The Major bought them off. How come you and Curly stayed?"

The man shifted from one foot to the other. "A deal's a deal," he said. "I ain't much at changing sides."

Cosgrave looked at him for a moment in silence, then stepped into the corral.

Shay said, "You still going?"

He caught the horse before he answered. When he came out leading it, he said: "Those cows rightfully belong to me, no matter what my uncle does. I'm not going to let Dude Rankin run off with them, not if I can stop him."

"You going alone?"

The Polsen boys had moved up behind Shay and stood listening. The taller said, "Want some help?"

The question caught Jet off guard. He turned to look at them, his tired face lighting. "I could use some, but what about your brother?"

The tall one said: "Nothing we can do for Olf. Maybe he'd like the idea that we're riding with you."

Cosgrave had long since given up hope of understanding the mountain people. He nodded and moved over to the house.

Olf Polsen stirred in the bunk and opened his eyes when Jet bent over him. He said weakly, "I can't figure you out."

"Nothing to figure," said Jet, pulling away the crude bandage and replacing it. "That hole's clean. You've lost a lot of blood, but if you take it easy . . ."

"I ain't going to make it." Polsen showed no emotion. "I ain't got enough blood left to live."

Jet could think of nothing to say. Polsen was like a hurt animal, past the point of struggle, of caring. "The boys are going to ride with you. I wish I could go myself. That was white, the way you pulled those jaspers off me after I downed your horse." He was silent, picking at the frayed edge of the blanket with listless fingers. "Judy," he whispered.

"I've sent for her," said Jet, and watched the man's eyes close wearily. He turned away and found Olf's brothers lined against the wall behind him. They stood for a moment, staring in silence at Olf, then turned and filed out. A moment later he followed, moving toward the cookshack.

He and the Polsens ate in silence, without hunger or relish, knowing that they needed full strength for the ride ahead. When they finished he told Shay:

"Try the wounded men on coffee. Olf can't take much but the others will. The doctor should be here in five or six hours. There's not much you can do until he comes. We'll be back when you see us."

He walked away and swung into the saddle. The Polsens were already mounted, and they turned up the valley as the sun dropped down behind the screening trees on the west.

20

Four miles above the ranch,
Newmark Valley narrowed until it became in reality a
canyon. Up this the trail they were following climbed
along a rocky shelf which at times was a hundred feet wide,
at others scarcely twenty. To their right the river tore frantically downward, white water here, fighting its way over
boulders and jutting stony arms.

Along the trail they found full evidence that Rankin and
his men had already had their difficulties with the herd.
At the narrowest point three steers had gone over the bank,
killing themselves on the jagged rocks below. Their bodies
lay half in, half out of the rushing water. About a mile
farther on, the trail widened again, crossed the west fork
at a shallow ford, and climbed over the hogback to join the
trail in the Main Beldos Canyon.

The dust still hung in the air, churned up by a thousand
hoofs, although it was a good twelve hours since Rankin
had passed. Though the sun was entirely gone, and night
had settled on them suddenly as it does in mountain places,
Cosgrave did not hurry. There was only one place where
Rankin could bed down so large a herd: the mountain
meadow below Lone Star. It was a natural amphitheater,
with good grass and water, and it was the last real feed that
the cattle would find until they had crossed the summit and
reached the lush meadows of the Moccasin.

Had Cosgrave been making the drive, he would have
stopped to rest the stock and settle the herd before he
pushed on up the steep canyon trail. But Rankin would not
wait. Rankin wanted to get out of the country, fearing perhaps that the Major might change his mind and refuse to
honor the bill of sale that Prince had given.

Jet did not think that Rankin feared him. The trail boss

probably thought he was dead; at least, Sawyer's chance remark led Cosgrave to suspect that the Circle C had been warned by the trail boss that Jet was pulling out, perhaps that he had gone alone to Colton.

The click of an iron shoe on the rocks behind him reminded him that he was not alone. Behind him rode the Polsens, silent yet steady. It was ironical that they should ride to help recover Circle C stock. He speculated on their reasons for following him and he doubted that either man actually felt gratitude. Probably it was a matter of pride, a return for his help to Olf, an effort to repay an obligation which they felt. He knew that they still did not like him and that they probably never would, but he also knew that they would fully back his play. The mountain people never did things by halves. If they started with him, they would ride through no matter what happened in the canyon above.

It was a loyalty such as he had once felt for his own family. He thought that he might not have hated the Major so thoroughly now had he not idolized the man during the years of his childhood. He had been taught to believe that the Cosgraves were better than their neighbors, that the Circle C was the most important ranch in the country. His father had fostered that idea, and his father had died protecting the ranch. Now, he and his uncle were fighting, tearing the ranch apart, using its herds to bribe men like Rankin and Prince to murder. The Polsens would be glad to see the ranch die. To them it was a grasping octopus, always reaching out, always swallowing more range. Yet tonight they rode at his back, the only support he now commanded. Three men against a dozen; bad odds, and yet they never questioned them. He felt a warmness for the brothers that was not gratitude; it was deeper than gratitude. Recalling how he had once hated them, this puzzled him. Something was wrong with life when enemies turned friends and relatives ordered your murder.

As he caught the first gleam from the crew's camp fire, he forgot everything save the problem at hand. It was past midnight when he reined his horse and sat still in the middle of the trail, listening to the muted sounds from the herd, to the night riders as they slowly circled their charges, singing a low toneless chant to still the restless steers. Beyond the river lay the mining town, and the steady beat of its distant stamps carried from the mills in an undertone that mingled with the sound of rushing water.

Cosgrave turned to glance at his companions, saying in a low voice: "I'm going to ride in. Stay back, but cover me, and be certain not to come into the circle of the firelight."

They did not answer, and he urged his horse forward, every sense alert, knowing that their greatest hope lay in surprise. Silently he pushed on, making directly toward the shadowed chuck wagon, surrounded as it was by the blanketed forms of the sleeping crew. As he advanced a figure rose from the wagon tongue, walked to the fire, and lifted the blackened coffeepot. He filled a cup, raised it to his lips, and at that moment heard Cosgrave's horse. He swung around.

"Who's there?"

The voice was not Rankin's. Cosgrave rode in boldly. It was the only way to play it, boldly.

The man's voice caught an edge of panic. "Who is it? Sing out."

"It's me," said Cosgrave, and pushed his mount into the circle of firelight. "What's the matter, Davis, spooky?"

The man's hand lay on the stock of his belted gun, and the sleeping men were stirring, throwing aside their blankets. Cosgrave noted that there were six of them. Rankin was not there. Jet made no move to dismount. From the saddle he could watch them all as they came out of sleep.

The man by the fire asked the question for all of them. "What do you want?"

He laughed then, without mirth. "What would I want? My cattle. You'll turn the herd back at daylight."

"Rankin has a bill of sale for them."

"Where's Rankin?"

Davis made a sweeping gesture toward the distant town. "Over there, with the Indian agent. They're making a dicker."

"He's got nothing to sell. These steers are mine."

Jet felt the weight of their fear and their dislike. He knew how very dangerous they were, and he was glad that the Polsens were in the shadows with their ready guns. As he wheeled his horse away, from the corner of his eye he caught the movement as Davis drew his gun. He would have been too late, but behind him a rifle flashed and Davis fell headlong into the fire, scattering the burning brands. The other riders, still a little drugged from sleep, stood rooted in their places, not moving as Cosgrave swung back, gun in hand, and dropped lightly to the ground. With his free hand he seized Davis's shoulder and dragged the fallen man out of the fire. The shirt was already smoldering, and Cosgrave beat it out with his hat; but he need not have bothered, for Davis had been shot through the head.

Jet straightened, meeting the stony stare of the crew and hearing the pound of hoofs as the nighthawks came rushing away from the cattle to learn the meaning of the shots. Then Cosgrave heard another sound, a sound that chilled his blood. The herd was stirring. He knew that nothing in the world was as suspicious and untrusting as a steer; that a steer could see disaster in a flash of lightning or a rolling tumbleweed, or hear it in a gun shot, transmitting his terror to his fellows by merely turning his head.

All over the bed ground the cattle were shifting uneasily, and if they needed further cause for panic they had it as a charging nighthawk saw Cosgrave beside the scattered fire and thew a bullet at him. The bullet missed, plowing into the canvas-topped chuck wagon. Both Polsens shot in return, their rifles sending out their sparks of rim fire into the night. One bullet caught the charging rider; the second whined away to strike among the restless cows. With the shots the men about the fire faded back into the darkness and their bullets hammered at Jet, one killing his horse, another tearing through his shirt between his body and his arm but without breaking the skin. He turned, diving out of the light, covered by the Polsens' smacking guns. As he turned he heard the cattle on their feet, moving uncertainly. In another moment the run had started.

They came slowly at first, their odor of fear spreading acridly before them, bawling their nameless terror. As their speed increased, Jet knew that he stood directly in their path. Suddenly the Polsens loomed out of the darkness, one on either side; the tall man kicked a foot out of the stirrup, reaching down to help Cosgrave swing up. Then they were driving for the river and the town beyond. Behind them the first wave of rushing animals hit the camp, trampling out the last of the fire, upsetting the chuck wagon and pouring on.

Cosgrave had no time to think of the riders who had been sleeping there only moments before. He glanced back, seeing the front row of maddened animals. There was no hope of checking them; a hundred riders could not have halted that stampede. He felt the horse under him quiver at its double load, and knew that the race would be close. Suddenly they slid down the cutbank and were in deep, chilling water. He flung off, trying to avoid the horse's kicking hoofs, and swam, letting the current carry him downward and across toward the other bank. Finally grounding, his lungs half filled with water, he dragged himself up the slippery rocks to safety.

The Polsens stayed with their horses, swimming them through the swift water and landing below him, somehow getting the frightened animals across the rocks to the firmer footing above. They called and he limped toward them, turning his head to watch the surging herd. It was veering in a wide sweep that would carry it into the mouth of the lower canyon and down the treacherous trail he had just climbed. But the near flank struck the stream's edge, and some luckless animals were driven over the bank, pushed by the avalanche behind them. They plunged down into the river, kicking, struggling, breaking themselves on the jagged rocks. Their bawling and the bawling of the running mass filled the night. Their hoofs made dull thunder and beat up dust to choke the air.

Beyond them, he heard scattered shots, and he judged that some night rider was vainly trying to turn the cows. Nothing could have checked the fear-crazed animals. The mass rolled on and on, seen faintly in the light from the distant moon, a confused blur of pitching backs and horns, a sea of bodies rushing inevitably toward its own destruction on the wicked curves of the canyon trail. Half, no, more than half of those animals would be crushed to death in the bloody stream bed before the hour was out. The thought sickened him, and he turned to walk to where the Polsens were resting their wet horses. A sudden warning shout made him spin about.

Two horsemen were charging toward him from the small mining town. He guessed at once that one of them was Rankin, and all the rage that had gripped him during the long ride flooded up to fill his tired body. This man had sold him out, had accepted a deal and had then double-crossed him by dealing with the Major. Had Rankin stayed at the Newmark house, Cal Prince's crew would not have had their chance to attack. If it had not been for Rankin, the cows that were dashing themselves to death in the canyon below would be alive, spread peacefully through the hills. Rankin was shouting: "Who is it? What happened? Sing out."

"It's me," said Cosgrave, his voice carrying above the pound of the running herd and the rush of the stream. "You'll never sell that herd, Dude. They're scattered from hell to breakfast."

Rankin jerked his horse to a stop. "Damn you, Cosgrave; those animals were mine. I've got a bill of sale."

"Not from me. Show your bill of sale to the steers. Wave it in their dead faces."

The man swore again. "I'm not through," he called. "As soon as I gather the crew, I'm coming back for another herd. We won't ride out empty-handed."

One of the Polsens ended the talk by throwing a rifle shot that kicked up dust at the feet of Rankin's horse. The animal swerved violently and charged back toward town with Rankin fighting it. The man with him fired a useless shot over Cosgrave's head and fled after Rankin's plunging horse.

Both Polsens started to mount but Jet ran toward them

shouting, "Let me have a horse, damn it; let me have a horse."

Sven said sharply, "We'll go with you."

"Stay here," Jet ordered. "The rest of the crew may try to cross the river and box us. You keep them off. I'll handle Rankin."

"Let him go." It was the younger boy.

Cosgrave looked at him, then turned to Sven again. "You heard what he said. Dude Rankin means exactly what he says. He'll come back and I'll have my hands doubly full, the Major on one side, Rankin and my old crew on the other. I've got to settle this tonight." He had already caught the reins from the boy's hands and swung up. "If I don't come back in an hour, shove off for home." He turned then and rode toward town, his eyes alert for any sign of movement. He had an idea that Rankin would not have gone far. It was not in the man's make-up to run.

Lone Star was a poor town, a company town, owned by the mine to house its workers. There were two saloons with one hotel facing them across the width of Texas Avenue. Someone with a sense of humor had named the street, for it was not an avenue and it was a good four hundred miles from Texas; but to Jet Cosgrave there was no humor in the place.

He halted his horse once to allow two ore wagons to pass, then rode slowly forward, keeping in the shadow of the dark buildings. Nothing broke the stillness except the thunder of the stamps, and he doubted if the town had heard the stampede above the noise from the mill. The streets were deserted, and it was possible, though improbable, that Rankin and his companion had ridden directly through.

He rode up before the hotel, stepping from the horse so that its thick body offered him a partial shield as he scanned the empty street. Lights glowed from the windows of both saloons. Suddenly a sound behind him made him turn, and he saw Rankin push the hotel door partly open. For a breathless instant they faced each other, neither speaking, neither wanting to be the first to reach for his belted gun.

21

It was Rankin who broke the
waiting, Rankin who moved first. With an oath his hand
swept down fanwise, the fingers spread. Jet saw him move
and threw himself sidewise, dropping to one knee, hearing
Rankin's bullet strike a porch post.

Jet's first shot knocked the glass from the upper panel
of the door and his second clipped the jamb; then he
whirled, seeking shelter. The movement saved his life, for
the man who had been riding with Rankin stepped around
the corner of the hotel and fired twice, both bullets missing
Cosgrave and striking the horse. It screamed, plunging
ahead, its front feet pawing at the air, almost striking Cosgrave as he leaped out of the way. Its body blocked the
hotel door and spoiled Rankin's chance, then it leaped
along the building front, straight at the second man. He fell
sideways, avoiding the beating hoofs. As he tried to rise,
Cosgrave shot him twice, then hurdled the body and swung
quickly around the corner of the hotel.

He never knew whether the fallen man was a member
of the crew or the Indian agent with whom Rankin had
been dickering, and he had no time to find out and no interest in knowing. His attention was on the trail boss, hiding
inside the building. He paused, breathing deeply, knowing
that if it had not been for the accident of the plunging horse
one or both of the men would have killed him. They had
planned the maneuver, one inside, talking to hold his attention, while the other crept up to the corner on his flank.
But the odds were evened now, he against Rankin; and
while the trail boss had the shelter of the building, Jet was
free to move about.

He rested, listening, and heard nothing but the endless

hammer of the stamps. Either the citizens of Lone Star were too used to gunfire to let it disturb them, or the pounding from the mill had deadened the sound of the shots. His sole concern was Rankin. Somewhere beyond the thin shake wall the man waited, deadly as a coiled snake. It was a question of who would guess right in this earnest game of hide and seek. He replaced the spent loads in his gun, then followed the line of the building toward the rear, welcoming the deepening shadows which served to screen him.

The best thing would have been to wait where he was, to make the trail boss come to him; but in him was a driving impatience that would not allow him to remain motionless. He had just reached the corner of the building when he saw the hotel's back door pushed cautiously open. He knew that his man was peering out into the darkness of the alley. Jet stooped, found a rock the size of an orange, and heaved it across the alley against the boards of the facing building. It struck with a clatter and Rankin fired twice, keeping masked within the doorway so that he was not visible to Jet. Cosgrave waited, hoping that the man would venture out to see the effect of his shots; but the trail boss was too cagey to expose himself.

They stood thus for a full minute of utter silence, then Rankin's voice called roughly: "Speak up, Cosgrave. Speak up."

Jet made no sound. He turned and slipped along the wall until he reached the street line, then moved along it to the hotel entrance, which he pushed open. Still screening part of his body behind the door, he peered the length of the hall and saw Rankin at the other end. He shot once and heard the man's startled oath, but knew instinctively that he had missed as Rankin vanished into the alley. Jet hesitated for an instant; then, instead of running back around the building, he retreated across the street, taking up his position in the shadow of the far building line.

He waited there so long that he thought the man must have slipped away. His shirt was sweaty from his effort, and the mountain wind sweeping down the canyon was chill. He shivered a little in its draft as he studied the empty street. There was something ghostly and unreal about the deserted town. It was as if he and Rankin had the whole world to themselves. The lights of both saloons had gone out, and he guessed that whoever was in the bars stood at the windows watching him. It gave him an uncomfortable feeling, and he moved back, desiring a darker shadow.

His eyes strained as they raked the hotel, until he began to imagine movement where there was none. He knew that this was only the tautness building up in his tired body, the pressure of waiting closing in on him. He thought: Now I know what a man's mind does while he's waiting for death. Curiously, his mind seemed almost empty. He tried to think of his uncle but failed to picture him. He tried to figure what he would do next but found that it was of little importance. Only Rankin was important at that moment; only the knowledge that the man was somewhere across the street, stalking him in the darkness as if he were some dangerous animal.

Rankin could have reached a horse and ridden out. There was that possibility, yet Rankin was not the kind to run. A man like Rankin had nothing but his pride. He would wait and watch for an opportunity to strike, but he would not run. Knowing this, Jet watched the hotel, the shadows around it, and the now dark rectangle of the window. He knew that this was a game of patience, that the loser would be the one who grew impatient first, the one who grew reckless and exposed himself by a false move.

It was Rankin who lost. In being too clever he lost, for somehow he had managed to climb to the hotel roof. Jet could not know how long the man had lain there, watching, waiting for some move of Jet's to expose his position. But Jet did not stir. He stood, his shoulders braced against the wall of the store, its wooden awning blocking out what little light there was, his eyes centered on the hotel door.

It was an old trick: to fix one object in the center of your vision and to watch everything before you from the corners of your eyes. The awareness of Rankin's position came slowly. He saw a little darkened mound breaking the straight line of the hotel roof. Afterward Jet knew that he must have seen the man seconds before his mind realized the significance of what he saw. Not until Rankin stirred, standing half erect the better to see the street, was Jet sure. Then he raised his gun carefully, deliberately, and fired.

His shot hit the man squarely. Rankin spun and then fell backward to the roof, his big body concealed by the heavy coping. Even then he was not through; for he dragged himself to the edge of the parapet and managed to empty his gun, his bullets shattering the window on Cosgrave's right. Jet fired again. He saw Rankin lean forward and then tumble downward, crashing through the hotel awning to land heavily in the dust below.

Jet walked slowly forward, his gun held ready. The big trail boss lay twisted, his dust-covered figure limp as a boneless bundle of old clothes. Jet bent down and found no sign of life, then turned, examining the street, for not all the crew had been caught by the stampede. But there was no sign of anyone. Lone Star had no marshal and no law except the authority of the mining company. He turned away, walking down the street to where two horses stood at a hitching rack. Looking at their brands, he knew that these had been Rankin's and his man's.

Mounting and leading the second horse, he rode out toward the river, finding the Polsens waiting where he had left them. No one spoke. The tall brother mounted the spare horse, and without a word they swung down toward the canyon.

The moon had reached the zenith of the sky, and its light showed them the havoc which had been wrought by the charging herd. At each turn broken animals were piled against the walls or had fallen over into the stream bed, their carcasses grotesque and unreal in the half-light. Jet rode automatically, ignoring the signs of slaughter, his horse shying a little but following the Polsens. It was an old habit of the long trail, to sleep thus in the saddle, with your eyes wide open but your mind a blank.

They came down the canyon, crossed the hogback, and

dropped into Newmark Valley. As they rounded the wooded point, they saw the lights from the ranch far below them. Shay challenged them from the darkness as they approached the yard, and Cosgrave came awake to answer him. They rode on, into the path of light, and found Eaton smoking beside the house door.

Cosgrave stepped down and asked in a low tone, "How is it, Doc?"

Eaton threw away his cigar. "Polsen's dead. He'd lost too much blood before I got here. Some day they'll figure how to carry extra blood around in bottles."

The brothers came up at Cosgrave's side, and at the doctor's nod they filed quietly into the room. They walked over to the bunk and looked down at the blanketed shape. They did not turn back the blanket to expose Olf's face nor did they look at each other. They simply stood there, without saying anything. Then, as if by common consent, they swung and came back through the door, walking to their horses.

Cosgrave said, "There'll be coffee in the cookshack."

They both looked around at him. "Thanks," said Sven. "We'll go home and get the wagon for Olf." They mounted and rode silently out of the yard, not looking back.

He thought tiredly: I didn't thank them. They covered me tonight, just as they saved us this afternoon, and I didn't thank them.

It came to him that his debt to the Polsens was stretching out. Whatever else you thought of them, they were good hands to ride with, loyal and unswerving. The thought brought Judy to mind, and for the first time in hours he remembered that he had sent Curly for her. Cosgrave called to Shay, who had unsaddled his horse and came across the yard. He angled over and asked with mild curiosity, "Find Rankin?"

"I found him," said Cosgrave. "The herd stampeded down the canyon. A good half of them are dead."

Shay was enough of a cowman to feel real regret. "A hell of a waste," he said. "And Rankin?"

"Dead." Cosgrave looked toward the cookshack. "Anyone come out with the doctor?" His mind was on Judy.

"Three women," Shay said. "They're in the cookshack, keeping warm. I guess they didn't hear you ride up."

"Three women?" Cosgrave masked his surprise. He turned and walked quickly over the uneven ground. Judy would be there, and Nan Ireland probably, since she often helped the doctor, but who else?

He came against the closed door and thrust it open. The first person he saw was Judy; the second, Alice Austin; and then he saw his uncle and felt an actual physical shock, as if they had come together jarringly. Neither spoke, yet neither dropped his eyes. It was as if each was afraid to be the first to look away.

22

For a moment Jet Cosgrave
stood blocking the cookhouse door, and in that moment
every motion within the room ceased. Curly froze, the coffeepot half raised, almost in the act of pouring the black
liquid into Nan Ireland's cup.

It was Nan Ireland who broke the tension. "You've got
visitor's, Jet."

"So I see." His full attention remained on the Major. He
wanted to speak to Judy, to tell her that he was sorry about
Olf; but his uncle standing there was a black shadow cast
across the whole gathering.

He said slowly: "I didn't expect you in the Newmark,
Major. This ground hasn't been healthy for the Circle C."

Slow color mounted into Linton Cosgrave's face. It was
with obvious effort that he controlled his anger enough to
speak.

"Maybe I should have come sooner. Maybe the fight
would have gone differently had I been present to direct it."

"That," said Jet, "is something we'll never know. You've
failed, Major. You sent Prince and your men against us
twice, and half your crew is dead. You tried to bribe Dude
Rankin, and he's dead."

The Major said quietly, "And the herd he took—"

"Part of it's dead also. They stampeded down the canyon. I ask you again what you are doing here?"

The Major's eyes strayed for a moment toward Alice
Austin, and it was she who spoke.

"He came here to find me," she said. "I was with Nan
Ireland when your man came, seeking Judy, and I came
out to help. The Major followed from town when he
learned where I'd gone."

Jet looked at her and then at the Major, reading hate deep in the older man's eyes. He thought: The Major came here because he was jealous. He's not forgotten that I spent the night sheltered in her room. He'll never forget, and he'll never forgive me. He hates me more than he did before, far more. It is one more thing between us. If the women weren't here, he would have drawn his gun.

Aloud he said, "I thank you for coming, as I thank Nan Ireland and the doctor; but the Major is not welcome, and will not be welcome as long as I hold the Newmark." He turned then and stepped out into the darkness of the yard, striding toward the main house. He met Dr. Eaton in the door, and the doctor pulled him into the light.

"Let me have a look at you."

"I'm all right," said Jet. He swayed a little and leaned one hand on the rough wall for support.

"Sure," said the doctor sourly. "You're all right. You're punchdrunk with fatigue, but you're all right."

Jet's voice cut at him. "What did you bring the Major here for?"

The doctor stared at him and then chuckled, without mirth. "I've been accused of many things in my life, Jet, but never of bringing the Major anywhere. Your uncle goes where he pleases, how he pleases."

"Not on my land," said Jet. "I'm going to break him, Doc."

"Maybe," said Eaton. "Maybe you will. He quarreled with the Austin girl tonight. They quarreled about you. I couldn't help overhearing."

Jet waited.

"And something else," said Eaton, his eyes on the younger man's face. "Judy heard."

Jet didn't answer.

"I just thought you'd like to know." Eaton was like an old woman in his love for gossip.

Jet said: "You can do two things for me, Doc. Go over to the cookshack and ask Judy to step out, and then get the Major off the place before I kill him."

Eaton shook his head. "You Cosgraves. I'd hate to be between you."

"Go on," said Jet, impatience creeping over the weariness in his voice. "Go on."

Eaton shrugged and moved toward the cookshack. In a minute Judy appeared and Jet called to her. She crossed to the main house slowly, and he tried to take both her hands. She pulled quickly away.

"Let me alone."

He stared at her in the half-light. He was so very tired that it was almost all he could do to stand. "What's the matter with you?" His voice was rougher than he intended.

"Nothing's the matter with me." There was anger in her tone. "I guess I was a fool, that's all; and no one likes to be a fool."

"What are you talking about?"

It was not in her to dissemble. "Jet, you and I weren't intended to be anything to each other, not even friends. I made a mistake. No one ever kissed me before, not like that; and I thought it meant more than it did."

He had a sudden helpless feeling of not being able to reach her, not being able to make her understand; yet tired as he was, he felt that he must try.

"Listen to me," he said. "Dr. Eaton said that he and you overheard the Major quarreling with Alice Austin about me. I don't know what was said, but—"

"Enough. I don't blame you, Jet. She's pretty, she's beautiful. She's everything I'm not and . . ."

He was at the end of his patience, almost at the end of his strength. "All right, I kissed her. I'll even admit that for the moment it occurred to me that a way to strike at the Major was to try and take her away from him. But I was wrong. I knew it tonight when I rode up the trail with your brothers at my back. I knew it when I stepped into the cookshack and saw you there. It's you I want, Judy. I never wanted anything else."

She turned away from him, as if refusing to listen. He said in desperation: "Wait. You haven't asked about your brothers. They're all right. They came down with me. They've gone home but they'll be back by morning."

She continued to move away. He took a step, as if to follow her, then stopped as the cookhouse door opened and the others appeared.

Eaton said: "You harness my team, Major. Damn it, a doctor should have some rights." Then he came toward Jet: "I'll leave the two wounded Circle C men here tonight. The Major can send for them in the morning."

Jet nodded without speaking, and Nan Ireland crossed toward Judy. "Are you ready?"

The girl said in a low voice: "I'll stay here. My brothers will be back by morning."

The dressmaker hesitated, then turned toward the buckboard and allowed the doctor to help her in. Eaton shook the reins. With the two women in the rear seat he swung out of the yard and took the road to town, the Major following on horseback.

23

The ride to town was made
for the most part in silence. Alice Austin had little to say,
and Nan Ireland hardly opened her mouth. The Major
trailed them, riding a hundred yards behind the rig. It
amused Eaton to see the man's sullen face when they pulled
up before the hotel.

The Major helped Alice Austin down then offered his
hand to Nan Ireland, but the dressmaker shook her head.
"I'll make Doc drive me home."

They covered the distance without speaking. It was not
until he had helped her to the ground before her own gate
that Nan Ireland asked, "What'll happen to Judy Polsen
now?"

Eaton shrugged. "Who knows. Who knows what happens to any of us?"

"She's young," said the woman, "and the young take
things seriously. Do you think Jet will marry her?"

He countered by saying: "Do you think Jet will live?
The Major isn't through yet."

"No," said Nan Ireland and turned in to the house. The
doctor stood where he was for a moment, then climbed
slowly to his seat and drove to the livery. His team stabled,
he moved on down to the Palace saloon, noting several
horses with the Circle C burned into their flanks. He hesitated. If Cal Prince and the remaining members of the
Major's crew were inside, they'd be in a bad humor. He
almost decided that he did not want his drink, then he
turned, glancing up the almost empty street.

Mather, the marshal, was standing in the shadow at the
corner, and Sam Allen sat in one of the cane-backed chairs
before the Banner House. Both men were too casual; and

Eaton, who knew the town so well, sensed that they were watching the saloon, that they were waiting for trouble. As he hesitated, the Major came from the Colton corner, cut diagonally across the thick dust, and without a word of any kind brushed past the doctor and pushed through the swinging doors into the long room beyond.

Curiosity made Eaton follow. As soon as he stepped inside, he saw the Circle C men ranged along the bar. The Major had come to a stop beside them and was talking to Cal Prince in a low tone. The room was not crowded. It was very late, and already Ted Alba, the owner, had turned out the window lamps. Alba was big, and quiet, and middle-aged. Years of running saloons had taught him caution and understanding. Across his bar he served everyone impartially and took no part in the small quarrels and jealousies that divided the town.

He stood now behind the counter, leaning his hips against the edge of the back bar, watching the two bartenders on duty and giving no apparent attention to the small tight group of Circle C riders. But Eaton knew that Alba, for all his apparent disinterest, was watching every move made by the Major's men.

Cal Prince was drunk, sullen, and morose. He listened to what the Major said, his red-rimmed eyes shifting continually around the room. Eaton pressed up to the bar. He heard the Major's low voice and sensed the burning anger underneath the words.

"We're not through yet," the Major was saying. "He got the herd back, what's left of it; but he has no crew, only one man and a cook, and he won't get more. The Polsens rode with him tonight and they may back his play, but otherwise he's alone."

Prince glanced at his remaining men. "We aren't so well off ourselves."

"Pick another crew," the Major told him. "Pay double wages if you have to, and don't get in trouble here in town."

"I'm all right," said Prince.

"You're drunk," the Major told him. "You'd better hit the road for the ranch. I'm staying in, at the hotel." He turned then, again brushing past Eaton without seeing him, and left the saloon.

Prince stared after him, half angrily, his natural belligerence whetted by the liquor he had drunk. "I'd like a crack at young Cosgrave, all by myself, with no one around to stop us." He turned back to the bar and refilled his glass from the bottle. "I should have nailed him when he first came in. Bert wanted to; Bert would have taken him." He threw off the drink and looked around the room, brooding. "Him and that fat salesman come up toting the bags for the Major's girl—" He stopped, his attention directed toward one of the card tables at the rear of the long room. He pushed himself away from the bar and started toward the tables.

One of his riders tried to stop him. "The Major said—"

"Hell with the Major." Prince shook himself loose and moved unsteadily toward one of the tables where George Pitman sat with his back to the bar. He had been playing since early evening, and luck had run against him. The salesman was so intent on recovering his losses that he paid no attention to anything around him. He was not even aware that Prince was in the saloon until the foreman came against the table, between two seated players.

"On your feet, fatty."

Pitman looked up, startled. "Why, what—"

"Friend of Jet Cosgrave's, aren't you? Come in on the same train."

Pitman's heavy cheeks sagged and his small eyes clouded with quick fear. He forgot all about the money he had lost. His single impulse was to rise, to get away from there, but his legs refused to answer the message from his brain. He sat stupid and unmoving. The other men at the table had come out of their chairs, and the fat man found himself alone, the table between him and Prince. And then he was robbed of that barrier, for Prince reached down, his big arms spread-eagled as he caught the rounded edges of the table. He picked it up easily, as if it had no weight, and heaved it sideways into another table, knocking a man from a chair as he attempted to scramble out of the way.

The eyes of the fat salesman were on the foreman's as if he were fascinated. Prince's were filled with gloating triumph. In attacking the salesman his fevered brain sensed an opportunity to strike at Jet Cosgrave. He could not have explained his reasoning. He did not really care. All his frustrated anger now centered on the helpless man before him as he pulled his gun.

"On your feet. Get up!"

Somehow, somewhere George Pitman found the strength to rise, to stand, trembling and unhappy.

"Okay," said Prince. "Now dance."

The fat man looked around the room despairingly. He found no help. Dr. Eaton's expression was one of distaste; the others seemed amused.

"Damn it," said Prince, "dance!" The gun in his hand exploded, the bullet cutting the floor between Pitman's feet.

The fat man danced. He had all the grace of a clumsy bear and none of the willingness. He danced until the sweat started out on his purpling cheeks and his breath was a rattling gasp in his throat.

"Dance!" Prince fired again. He backed to the bar, men giving way for his passage, and picked up a half-filled whisky bottle in his free hand. He took a drink from the bottle, then walked forward and shoved it at the still bobbing fat man. "Drink!"

George Pitman drank. He strangled, met Prince's goading eyes, and drank again, thoroughly, until the bottle was empty. He went to throw it aside but Prince stopped him.

"Stand it on your head." He raised his gun, showing what he meant to do.

Pitman tried. He was shaking so that the bottle wouldn't balance. Prince lost his remaining patience. He stepped in, grabbed the bottle from the man's trembling fingers, and swung it in an arc, shouting, "Maybe this will make it stay." He crashed the bottle down on Pitman's head, shattering the brown glass.

Pitman collapsed. He went forward onto his face without a sound and never moved. There was a gasp from the crowd; some of the amusement died and a rumbled protest grew. Prince let his hot eyes rake along the line, and the protest died.

He stalked to the bar. "Gimme another drink."

Ted Alba motioned his bartender aside and stepped forward unemotionally. "That poker table cost thirty dollars, Cal."

Without a word the foreman counted out the money. "Now gimme a drink."

Alba set a bottle before him. Prince drank from the neck, then turned and walked out of the saloon. His crew followed him.

Dr. Eaton stepped into the street. He saw Prince arguing with his crew; then the riders turned toward their horses while the foreman moved swayingly down the street. He passed Sam Allen, still seated in the chair before the Banner House, and vanished into the hotel. Eaton guessed that within five minutes Prince would be asleep. Satisfied, the doctor turned back into the saloon. No one had touched the fallen salesman. He bent down at Pitman's side, testing the pulse, then he straightened, looking at Alba. "Get a couple of men to carry him down to the hotel. He'll have nothing worse than a sore head in the morning." Not until Pitman had been lugged away did the doctor turn toward the bar. He was still leaning on its edge half an hour later, when gray light began to filter into the room.

Alba said irritably: "Why don't you go home? I'd like to close up some time."

"Why," said Eaton, "sleep only wastes your time." He picked up the bottle and walked out with dignity, a lonely man who hated to be by himself.

24

The noise of horses in the yard roused Jet. It was broad daylight, and the sun was beginning to show over the eastern rim. He had slept under a tree, and for a moment he lay quiet as the Polsen wagon turned into the yard, his muscles so stiff that any motion brought sharp pain. Finally he pushed the blanket aside and stood up.

Judy was in the doorway of the main house, her red hair mussed as if she had bent her head forward against her crossed arms. Shay had been sleeping beside the cookshack, where he still lay in his twisted blankets. Curly had apparently remained awake, for he was framed in the cookhouse door and blue smoke was rising in the quiet morning air from the battered chimney.

The Polsen wagon was old and unpainted but still sturdy. Old Hans sat in the center of the hard seat, his body ramrod straight, his useless legs wrapped in a blanket against the morning chill, his gnarled hands holding the reins. His sons were mounted, sitting their horses beside the wagon, calm and unhurried and taciturn.

Jet Cosgrave stretched, finding his right arm so stiff that he could not entirely straighten the elbow. The cut across his stomach must have sprung during the evening ride. He had not been conscious of it, but the bandage showed a line of fresh blood.

The wagon pulled to the center of the yard. The old man halted the team and sat motionless, staring at nothing. His sons were quiet, making no move to dismount.

Cosgrave limped toward them, making his greeting purposely brief. "Chuck must be about ready. Step down."

They dismounted then, having observed the etiquette of

174

the country. The old man did not stir or show that he had heard.

Judy left the main house and walked to the cookshack without looking at anyone. She disappeared past Curly, reappearing a few minutes later, a filled plate in one hand, a steaming cup of coffee in the other. She walked past Cosgrave without speaking, ignored her brothers, and held up the plate to her father, who had turned at her approach. For an instant he seemed to hesitate, then he wrapped the lines around the socketed whip and with a mumbled thanks took the plate and then the cup.

She turned away, and as she passed her brothers she said in a low tone, "Chuck's on," and returned to the cookhouse. They followed her wordlessly. Cosgrave watched them go, then moved to the main house.

Sawyer was awake, and Jet nodded to the wounded rider, got a fresh shirt and towel from his duffel, and moved out toward the river. There, behind some sheltering trees, he stripped and plunged into the icy water. It shocked the stiffness of his muscles and stung his open hurts, but it cleared his logy mind and brought the blood tingling to his skin. He rebandaged the cut across his stomach, dressed rapidly, and walked back to the yard, feeling a sudden quick hunger.

The old man still sat in the wagon, his used plate on the seat at his side, his twisted hand still holding the half-empty cup. His sons were eating, hunkered down on their heels, their plates held in their hands. Jet went by them and entered the shack to find Judy at the stove. She did not look up as he entered but passed him a filled plate in silence. He poured his own coffee, watching her as he did so; then, realizing that she did not mean to speak, he turned back into the yard and joined the Polsens.

Curly and Shay were a little apart, not hostile but showing no friendship for the eating men. No one spoke. The brothers finished and without a word laid their plates aside. They rose together, tramped to the house, and came out with Olf's blanketed body between them. They carried it across the yard carefully, placed it in the wagon, and then turned to their horses. Judy appeared, walked down to the corral and caught up her own mount. For an instant Cosgrave hesitated, then he walked to the wagon.

"Mind if I ride along?"

Old Hans did not speak, but Sven said in his soft voice: "We'd be proud to have you. Olf would like it too." They swung away then and Cosgrave turned to the corral.

Curly hurried to catch up with him, asking in a worried voice: "What about those jaspers in the house? What happens now?"

Jet said that he didn't know.

"There are still Circle C men left," Curly warned.

He knew that, but for some reason he did not seem to care. All the fight was washed out of him for the moment. He said: "If they come, ride for the brush. Maybe you'd better keep going. It might be healthier."

Curly's old eyes studied him. "Quitting, boss?"

He roused his thoughts, saying more harshly than he intended: "No, I'm not quitting, but from where I sit it looks as if we're playing a busted flush. There are only three of us. The Circle C's pretty well shot up, but there's nothing to keep the Major from recruiting another crew. Rankin stripped the cattle out of these hills. There's plenty left, but it would take a lot of time to gather them."

Curly jerked a thumb toward the departing Polsens. "What about them? They rode with you last night."

Cosgrave did not know. He did not even try to answer. He caught up a horse and mounted, but before he rode away he turned to say: "Take care of yourselves, you and Shay. Keep horses saddled and run for it if anyone shows up." Then he twisted his mount and spurred after the slow-moving wagon.

Judy rode a hundred yards behind her brothers. He reined in beside her, wanting to talk, but she gave no encouragement. She pressed her mount until it was even with Sven's, and the chance was lost. Cosgrave was forced to follow in their dust.

25

There was only a small crowd at the Polsen funeral. They gathered on the bleak hillside behind the unpainted building of the church and waited while the young minister opened his book and found the proper place. The wagon had been pulled close to the newly cut grave, and old Hans still sat erect on the seat, his weathered features showing no emotion. His sons stood beside the grave which Cosgrave had helped to dig, looking at nothing, seeming to hear nothing.

Sam Allen had driven up the hill in a borrowed buckboard, bringing Nan Ireland and Alice Austin. He stood now between the two women, resting his weight on his good leg, and Cosgrave saw that his hand was under Nan Ireland's arm. Judy stood apart, her head turned so that Jet could see only her profile. Her hat had slipped back, held only by the chin strap; and her hair was bare to the sun, which brought it alive with golden undertones. Her shoulders were straight and she showed no sign of grief.

As the minister's voice, deep and resonant as a reed organ, began the service, Cosgrave thought: How little good it is to make plans. Two weeks ago I had no idea that I'd be attending Olf Polsen's funeral. I had no idea that so many men would be dead, or that I'd have hurt Judy so deeply. I didn't plan it so. I planned a careful operation, taking my time, stripping the Circle C of cows, a few at a time, until I had goaded my uncle into a fight.

The fight had come and men had died, but he and the Major still lived. Both were without a crew, without fighting men; but both still lived, with the ranch between them, and five years of bitter hate which could not be erased. But somehow the pleasure of accomplishment had passed. The

177

mad desire to possess the Circle C had gone. He had killed for the ranch; and he had been ready to steal for it, to cheat to gain it. Yes, he had cheated, and he remembered Judy's anger, and her contempt.

He stood there watching her, not hearing the minister's words as the man paid the last tributes to the dead brother, not conscious of the desolate cemetery, of the weathered headboards, the untended graves. He was only conscious of a small girl standing straight and resolute and alone, and he knew suddenly that deep within him he had wanted her more than he wanted the ranch or the cattle or his revenge. And he'd lost her. The hill people were honest in their way, and they were hesitant in giving their trust. She had given him hers, and he had not had sense enough to realize what it meant. He had thrown it away for the cheap chance of hurting the Major, and he had little hope of winning it back.

Realizing suddenly that the service was over, he stepped forward to help lower the plain box into its last resting place. As he straightened, he found Judy's green eyes on him. For a moment he stared back at her before she turned away.

Sam Allen drove the women back down the hill, Judy quietly refusing her father's invitation to return home. Cosgrave stayed, helping the brothers fill the grave. After they had ridden out behind their father's slow-moving wagon, he walked back to town, with the young minister at his side. They said little, separated as they were by background, upbringing, and beliefs, but he felt a certain admiration for the man, knowing the hopeless struggle that he waged to maintain the church.

They parted at the edge of the business section and Jet moved on alone, coming into Fremont to find Sam Allen's buckboard halted before the Banner House while the printer spoke to Jim Banner. As Jet turned the corner, he saw his uncle come from the stairs beside the bank, with Delvine at his side, and move along the wooden walk to where the buckboard stood. Cosgrave paused. In his new uncertainty he had no real desire to face the Major, to see

Alice Austin again, or, for that matter, to see Judy at the moment, yet his stubborn pride would not let him avoid the meeting. It was inevitable; it was something from which he could not run.

He came forward slowly, his boots making their slight scuffing noise on the rough boards. He saw Delvine turn first, then speak to the Major. Lin Cosgrave had been beside the buckboard. He came around now, his mouth tight and hard, his lips compressed. Perhaps a dozen feet lay between them, but Jet did not stop. He came on, and as he came he thought: It's strange, but every time we meet, the girl is there. She stood between us at the hotel, and last night at Newmark. I wonder if she will halt us again today.

One look at the Major's face, however, was enough to brush this thought aside; for though Jet did not know it, his uncle had just asked Alice to step down, to talk things out with him, and she had refused.

"I've had enough of you," his uncle said, coming forward to meet him. "I want to break you with my hands. Shooting wouldn't be enough." He dropped his hand then, carefully, so that Jet could not misunderstand the move, and worked the buckle of his gun belt free, handing it to Delvine without taking his eyes from his nephew's face.

Jet nodded. He reached down, unfastened his own belt, and flipped the gun against the building wall. Yesterday he would have welcomed his chance to come to grips with the man he hated, but now he was no longer eager to fasten his fingers at the Major's throat.

Lin Cosgrave shucked out of his coat. He said: "I wish your arm wasn't crippled. I want no excuses after I've beaten you."

Jet understood fully. The Major had to prove himself; he had to prove himself with Alice Austin looking on. He had to show this city girl that in choosing his nephew she had chosen the lesser man. Jet recalled the look that Alice had given him in the cookshack on the preceding evening, and he thought: The Major's wrong. This girl has no interest in me. She might have had, for a moment, but the knowledge that I have ridden after the herd, that I have killed the man who stole it, has sickened her. She may not want him, but she most certainly has no interest in me."

He said aloud: "Don't let my arm bother you. If there is anything to worry about, it's your age."

There was a rawness in the way he said it. He lacked the Major's finished grace, and he knew the words would sting; for, though Lin Cosgrave was forty, he prided himself on his physical stamina.

They fought in the street, their boots churning up the dust until at times the watchers could barely see them. They fought as both had learned to fight, cruelly, without science, their only desire to hurt and hurt badly. Jet had lost his cool, detached feeling. From the first onslaught he realized that he was fighting for his life, that the Major would kill him if he could, maim him if it were possible.

The Major came in with both fists swinging, and Jet, handicapped by his almost useless arm, ducked away and drove his left fist in a looping hook that caught the Major's shoulder with such force that he was knocked off balance for a moment. Then the Major got in close, chopping his fists at Jet's kidneys. Jet thrust the man away, using his head and right arm for the push. Feeling quick pain from the strained arm, he arced his left around in a short punch that crashed against the Major's cheek between the jawline and the ear. He followed the blow with a second and then a third, hammering against his uncle's face, taking punishment in return as the Major's hard knuckles hit his damaged eye and re-opened the cut on his forehead. He lowered his head, blinded by the blood, and caught a heavy fist full on his ear. His head spun before he came in close against his uncle's shirt, spattered now with blood from Jet's face.

Jet sensed the knee coming up, pushed backward before it caught his groin, and grabbed the raised leg, upsetting the Major onto his back. Then he jumped on him in a woodsman's fall, his knees doubled close, driving them downward as he dropped with his full weight upon the older man's ribs. The Major's mouth came open as he gasped for air, and Jet, knowing no mercy, hit him twice in the face with his good hand before his uncle managed to roll over on his stomach and come to his hands and knees.

The younger man rolled with him, twisted, and half fell across the Major's back, locking his left arm around his throat, trying to pull his head backward, but the Major was too strong. He rolled again, throwing Jet heavily on his side. Jet fell with his right arm under him, cursing the pain and his lack of strength as he tried to rise.

The Major was quicker to come upright, and now he was astride his nephew, the positions reversed. He spread his strong fingers about Jet's neck and closed them with the relentless power of a steel spring. Jet gasped as the pressure cut off his air. He felt dizzy and saw a redness before his eyes. In desperation he brought up his left hand and tore frantically at the closing fingers. He got a hold on one of them and bent it back, but he was so far gone that he did not hear the bone snap and was only vaguely conscious that the Major had cried out with the sharp pain.

He rolled, more by instinct than design, and felt the Major's weight slip from his back. Somehow, he came to his feet. Through the haze, and through the blood which flowed down from the cut on his forehead, he saw the older man trying to rise. Jet swung his boot, almost upsetting himself, and felt the toe catch the Major's jaw, lifting the man and turning him over onto his shoulders in a half back-flip, groggy and almost senseless.

Jet jumped on him again, again using his drawn-up knees and driving them downward as he hit, repeating the woodsman's fall so viciously that he knocked the remaining air out of the older man. He heard the Major's whooshing groan, and fell sideways himself, catching his fall partly on his good arm, trying to rise again to his feet.

It seemed to take him hours to climb erect. He stayed crouched on his hands and knees for a full minute, half up, half down. He knew that the Major was stirring at his side, that he himself must get up, that the fight was not yet won; but he could not seem to get off his knees. Reaching out he wound the fingers of his good hand into the Major's yellow hair and sluggishly pounded his head against the street, but the thick dust cushion defeated his effort. Sensing this, he let go, rolling over and finally coming to his feet. He spread his legs, bracing himself, and stood swaying a little, his tortured lungs laboring for air. He tried to wipe the blinding blood from his eyes and sensed rather than saw that his uncle was rising. He stepped in and used the last of his strength in an uppercut that started from his boot tops and rose in a curving swing until it crashed squarely against the Major's face.

Had he missed, the momentum of the swing would have carried Jet from his feet, but he did not miss. His knuckles crashed against bone with such force that the middle one split and sent pain racing up his forearm. The Major's head snapped back as if his neck were broken. The force of the blow lifted him almost fully to his feet, then he fell slowly to land on his back, prone and unmoving in the dust.

Jet shook his head, trying to clear it. He took one step, then another, and caught the hitching rail. He turned, looking dazedly up and down the street, seeing the women motionless in the buckboard, every store doorway filled with its group of curious spectators. Then Cal Prince came around the corner of the Banner House and stepped into the middle of the street.

There was no doubting his intent. His face was twisted in a peculiar smile. He stopped, spread-legged, and everyone who saw him understood. Sam Allen was unarmed. He sat helpless on the buckboard seat. Andy Delvine had laid aside the Major's gun and had none of his own. They stood and looked, and could do nothing more.

Prince advanced slowly and stopped again, so that he could watch Allen and Delvine from the corner of his red-rimmed eyes. He said now in a low, even, mocking growl: "Get your gun, Cosgrave. It's there, on the sidewalk, next to the building."

Jet looked toward the gun. It was only a few feet away, but it might have been miles. He wasn't even certain that he could walk that far, and when he stooped to pick it up, would he be able to straighten? Certainly not fast enough to match Prince's speed. He was caught and there was no help for it, but he was too tired to care. He said in what he thought was a normal voice, but what sounded very like a croak, "Go ahead and shoot."

"No," said Prince, his lip curling from his yellow teeth. "I'll wait until the gun is in your hand."

"You damn' murderer."

Sam Allen moved convulsively and Prince snarled, "Keep out of this, cripple."

Judy had come to her feet, ready to jump down before the man, but Nan Ireland grabbed her arm, holding her back.

They were all standing thus when George Pitman appeared in the hotel doorway. His head was swathed in a white bandage and his fleshy cheeks were little darker than the cloth, but his pudgy hands held Jim Banner's shotgun, which he had taken from behind the hotel desk, and its twin barrels were pointed at Cal Prince. He didn't speak, and the foreman never saw him. The people in the buckboard were unconscious of his presence because they faced the other way. He held the gun so tightly that his fingers seemed numb; then he fired, discharging both barrels at once. The kick of the gun tore it upward from his grasp, the barrels almost smashing against his chin; but the shock of the double load caught Cal Prince fully in the side, tearing his big body open. He dropped as the echoes slapped the buildings, and the whole street swung, searching, and found the white-faced salesman leaning against the door jamb as if he had been stunned.

Andy Delvine recovered first, swinging about to catch up the Major's guns, but there was no need for them now. The old marshal and one of his deputies appeared, running out of Parker and along the walk.

Delvine said waspishly, "You always manage to turn up after the need for you is passed."

Mather refused to become excited. He said mildly: "I had a warrant for Jet. If I'd have come sooner, I'd have had to serve it. I figured to let them fight. I never thought about Prince."

They turned toward the unconscious Major, but Alice Austin was before them. She had dropped from the buckboard and, ignoring her trailing dress, knelt in the dust at the Major's side, lifting his battered head to rest it in her lap.

Allen stepped down and stamped toward Jet. "You all right?"

"All right," said Jet. He still leaned against the rail. "Hand me that gun, Sam. Some of the Circle C may be in town."

Allen got the gun. "I don't think so. They took off for the ranch last night. Both the Major and Prince slept in town." He turned as Dr. Eaton hurried up through the gathering crowd.

A dozen men were trying to help carry the Major into the Banner House and the marshal was having Prince's body removed. George Pitman had walked limply to a chair and collapsed. Judy and Nan Ireland were still in the buckboard, and Jet looked toward them, but both were watching the doorway of the Banner House.

He steadied himself for a moment, then limped to where George Pitman sat. "I owe you my life," he said.

Pitman's eyes were closed. He failed to open them, saying in a rough, uneven voice: "You owe me nothing, friend. I shot him for what he did to me." He was silent, trying to control his fluttering nerves. "It's strange. I never had the impulse to kill anyone before, and I'll not forget him, lying there. I'll see him every night before I go to sleep. But I'm not sorry. A man can only take so much, then he has to fight."

Jet turned away. A man had to fight, but what did fighting win? He had whipped his uncle. He could take the ranch and fight the law to hold it. Yet he felt empty, not proud. He had won a hollow victory.

Sam Allen took his arm. "You need some patching up," he said. "I'll take you down to Eaton."

Jet did not answer. He let himself be led away and limped on down the street, turning in to the doctor's office and waiting there for Eaton's return.

26

The afternoon's heat lay like a smothering blanket across the town, and men kept to the shade of the wooden awnings as they walked the street.

Jet Cosgrave sat in Allen's print shop, nursing his hurts and watching the red-haired boy building a castle in the deep road dust. Knowing that the castle would blow away with the first breath of wind, he thought: His building is just as permanent as mine. I planned something for five long years. I fed myself on bitterness and hate, living for the day when I could come home and beat the Major. I'm here, and I have beat him. Rankin is dead, and Cal Prince is dead, and the Major's hold is broken. Yet there's nothing left, nothing that I seem to want. And nothing much is changed.

He turned his eyes, looked at Allen tinkering with his usual doggedness at the old press, and said abruptly: "Stop wasting time, Sam. Go up to the Ireland house and tell Nan the way you feel. Do you think you're doing her a favor, hiding behind that peg?" Allen turned around, anger deep in his quiet eyes. "For a man who gives advice, you don't handle your own affairs very thoroughly."

"I know it," said Jet. "I had my chance and let it slip away. You're luckier than I am. You've had your chance for years and never taken it, but it's still there. For God's sake be a man; put on your hat and go up there. Get out of my sight before I murder you."

Allen looked at him, and some of the anger faded from his eyes. He grinned and without a word put on his hat. He was whistling as he started up Linden, moving faster than Jet had ever seen him.

The heat bore down. The shop was quiet now, and Jet's

185

sense of frustration grew. When Delvine appeared in the door, half blinded by the sun glare of the street, and stood for a moment accustoming his eyes to the dimness of the shop, Jet showed faint surprise. The little lawyer gave him a slow, calculated smile. "I've come to make a deal," he said, and stepped in to the high counter.

Jet's tone matched Delvine's. "I have no need of you, Uncle Andy. I've already won."

The lawyer's eyes turned bright with malice. "No," he said. "Stop to think a minute. What have you won? The Major's crew is dispersed, but he still holds legal title to the Circle C. Your original plan was to work from New-mark Valley and steal the cattle from the Major, blotting the brands to a double circle, but your crew is gone also. You can't steal too big a herd working alone."

"No," said Jet, and his voice showed how little real interest he felt. "It looks like a standoff."

"It's no standoff," said Delvine. "Unless you take my help, the Major still will beat you. I'll tell you what he plans. He's going to marry that city girl. Oh, I know that surprises you, but she's just agreed. She'll marry him if he promises to go east and stay there. She doesn't love him, but she thinks that the beating at your hands has taught him humility and grace." Delvine chuckled. "How very little she knows the Major. His plans are already made. He's going east on the evening train, and he'll marry her; but he'll also recruit a fighting crew. He'll send them here to take over the ranch, to run you out; and when everything is settled, he'll come back himself. That's how well you've won; you've won nothing but a continuing battle which will beat you in the end."

Jet had only been half listening to the words, but he said now, "If I've lost, why are you here, trying to deal with me?"

"Because," said Delvine in quiet triumph, "with me you have the Major whipped. Your father willed him the ranch, yes, but he also wrote a covering letter at the time, in his own hand, as an appendage to the will. That letter directed that when you were grown, when the threat from the hill people had been cared for, the Major was to deed the ranch back to you. Your father gave me the letter as a check on his brother, knowing that the Major might fail to keep the oral agreement they had already made."

"Go on." Cosgrave's tone had tightened with interest.

Delvine smiled a little, satisfied with the progress he was making. "The Major thought that I'd destroyed the letter, but I never destroy anything that might be useful. I only waited to see how strong you were, to see that if I put you in possession of the Circle C you'd be big enough to hold it."

"Where is the letter?"

Delvine drew it from his pocket and passed it over. "Don't think I'm trusting you too much," he said. " I trust no one; but without me to go into court as a witness to swear how and when that letter was written, the Major can fight it as a forgery."

Jet looked at the single page and saw that it was in his father's slanting hand. He asked one further question. "Where's the Major now?"

"At the Banner House," Delvine told him. "He and the city girl are there, waiting until it's time for the train."

Jet got up, but Delvine said: "Wait a moment. We haven't yet decided on my share."

Jet walked over and took his arm in one big hand. "You damn' cheat," he said tonelessly. "You can't even stay bought, can you? Come on. We're going down to see the Major." Anger erased his listlessness. "I don't like cheats. I tried to do a mean thing once, and it crossed me up. I've learned that it doesn't pay. I'm going to teach that lesson to you and the Major if I have to kill you both." His fingers tightened on Delvine's arm and he turned the struggling man from the shop and half pushed him up the street.

Lin Cosgrave sat in a chair beside the corner window of the rear room, the room which Jet had occupied on his first night in Colton. Alice Austin stood beside him, and they both turned with surprise when the door opened and Jet thrust the unwilling Delvine into the room.

The marks of the fight were plain on the Major's face,

but he had changed his clothes and his shirt was new and white and gleaming. There was surprise and anger in his eyes as he stared upward at his nephew saying, "Haven't you done enough?"

"Not nearly enough," said Jet, checking the impulse to laugh at the older man. "I brought something that belongs to you." He gave Delvine a contemptuous shove that sent the little lawyer over onto the bed. "You bought and paid for him, but he's showing signs of not staying bought. You should have run a brand on his hip."

The Major had never been a fool. He stared at his nephew, then at Delvine. Reading the guilt in the man's eyes, he said harshly, "What are you up to now?"

"He's selling you out," Jet said. "He came to me with the letter my father wrote along with the deed which turned the Circle C over to you."

"You're crazy," said the Major. "I never heard of any letter."

"You're lying," Jet told him calmly, and produced it from his pocket. "Shall I read it to you?" The Major did not answer. Alice Austin was staring from one man to the other. Jet said to her: "I understand you made a deal with him, that you would marry if he took you east and stayed there. Is that right?"

She nodded slowly.

He grinned. "Don't worry. I'm going to see that he keeps his bargain." He looked back at the Major and his face was stern. "I've learned a lot in the last week," he said slowly. "I came in here spoiling for a fight, burning with hate and bitterness. I know now that I chose the wrong way. Something's happened to me. Maybe I've grown up. I've learned that no one in life ever gets everything he wants. There has to be a compromise, and I'm offering one now. No, that's wrong. I'm telling you what you're going to do, and I'm going to make you do it.

"First, I want a quit-claim deed to half the Circle C. Second, I want a letter in your hand, promising that I shall have full management of the ranch and that you will never return to Colton. If you break that promise, your half of the ranch is to revert to me."

The Major tried to laugh. "And if I refuse?"

"Then you lose the whole ranch," Jet said savagely. "I almost hope you do. I'd like to take this letter into court and show your treachery to all the world. I can do it, too. The letter is in my father's writing, and Uncle Andy will testify when it was written and why." The Major looked questioningly at Delvine, but Jet gave the small lawyer no chance to speak. "He'll testify or I'll kill him. I don't think you need to have doubts on that score."

The Major's mouth turned down. He was a stubborn man, but he was also a fatalist. His decision was quick. "You win. Draw the deed, Andy. I'll write the letter." He looked curiously at his nephew. "I'm wondering why you chose to make this trade when you could have the whole ranch by going into court?"

Jet looked at Alice Austin and found her eyes upon him. He thought: I owe her something, and this pays her off. It means the Major will have to stay with her in the East and be the kind of husband she wants.

He did not explain, however, that for him, too, things were changed. When he'd come home, he'd been footloose, without responsibility; but now that the ranch was his, and the Major depended on his management for income, Alice would depend on him to keep her husband out of this country.

I've fixed things for others, he thought, pocketing the letter and the deed, but I don't seem to have found what I want, the contentment I thought I'd feel once I was home, once the ranch was mine.

He walked to the rear window and stood looking down at the alley and the livery barn beyond. As he stood there he saw Judy come along Linden, turn in, get a rope, and step into the corral to catch up her horse. She wore her blue denims and shirt and she had leaned her rifle against the fence. He stood watching her lithe movements as she put the loop on her horse, snubbed him, and slung the saddle up. Suddenly he bent down, stepped through the window to the kitchen roof, and dropped quickly to the alley below.

"Judy."

She looked around and saw him but she did not wait. If anything, she hurried faster, catching the rifle and swinging lightly into the saddle.

Cosgrave ran into the driveway of the barn. A horse was tethered there, already saddled. He did not even look to see what brand it was. He unfastened it and rode out into the street with a driving rush, ignoring Shorham, who waved frantically from the office as he passed.

Judy was already half a block into the residential section, riding steadily, not looking back, yet not driving her horse, as if she refused to give the appearance of running away. He wasted no time in shouts but drove his borrowed mount so that he caught her as she left the edge of town and climbed to the first row of hills.

"Pull up." He was at her side, but she gave no indication she had heard, keeping her face forward, holding her steady gait. He reached out suddenly and caught her rein, jerking her horse to a quick full stop. She turned on him then, her green eyes blazing, and tried to swing up the rifle. He caught the barrel, wrenched it from her grasp, and threw it as far as he could into the brush. She lashed at him with her quirt, the thong cutting across his cheek and bringing blood.

"You little devil." He pressed his horse against hers, using his knees. Slipping a hand around her waist, he lifted her clear of the saddle and set her on the ground. She didn't run as he flung down. She stood there facing him, her hands on her hips, her elbows wide, her hair tousled.

He said, "Judy, you've got to listen to me."

"I won't."

He caught her shoulders and pulled her to him, ignoring her struggles, encircling her arms with his superior strength. "You'll listen if I have to tie you. I never realized until last night what real loyalty is. Your brothers showed me. They helped me because I'd helped Olf, without hope of return, without caring what I did. All during the ride in from Lone Star, I thought about it. I thought about you, and I knew suddenly that the ranch didn't matter, that nothing meant anything if I did not have you."

She had stopped struggling, but she still held herself stiff and remote in the circle of his arms.

"It's over," he told her. "The Major and I will split the ranch, but its management stays with me. He's going east; he's going to marry Alice Austin."

That surprised her. "Jet!"

"No," he said. "You've got it wrong. I never wanted her, nor she me. A man doesn't deserve a second chance, Judy, but I want one. I know you love me, and I'm not going to let your hurt pride separate us."

She looked at him fully then, and he saw an awareness in her face which had not been there a few days ago. She too had learned and grown this week.

"All right, Jet. All right." She raised her lips for his kiss. She was still honest, still straightforward, making no pretense. As he held her to him, he knew the happiness that he had almost lost, and shivered to think how nearly he had missed it.

Later, standing arm in arm on the summit of the hill, they looked out across the town at the station platform, where the Major was assisting Alice Austin from old Jason's hack. From the west they heard the faint approach of the eastbound train. As they watched, the massive figure of George Pitman came out of the station and moved toward the track. Apparently the fat salesman was leaving, and suddenly Jet laughed.

When Judy looked at him questioningly, he said: "I was just wondering if that salesman would try to talk to Alice on the train, and if he does how jealous the Major will be. I think the Major has found his match in her. She'll attract men always, and the Major isn't young. It could turn him bitter."

Judy nodded soberly as the train pulled in to linger, puffing its impatience, while the passengers were loaded, the wood and water replenished. Then it pulled across the double bridge and took up its long looping climb to Traymore Pass and the distant East.

As if by common impulse, the man and girl turned to look at the western hills. The sun had already slipped from view, but its reflection still dyed the horizon a deep red.

Like blood, Jet thought. These hills had always known their share of blood, but he hoped that that would change. The need for fighting was finished. They would not quarrel with the hill people because in their minds they too were hill people, asking only to be let alone, to be allowed to live in peace.

He turned and looked down at the girl, and in her smile he read the same hope. For the first time in troubled years, he knew that he was fully content.

THE END